W9-ACJ-916

BLOOD FUGUE

SHIRLEY ESKAPA

Blood Fugue

Academy
Chicago
Publishers

Published in 1986 by

Academy Chicago Publishers
425 N. Michigan Avenue
Chicago, Illinois 60611

Copyright © 1981 by Shirley Eskapa

FIRST U.S. EDITION

Typesetting by Accent & Alphabet, Seattle

Printed and bound in the USA

No part of this book may be reproduced in any form without the
express written permission of the publisher.

Library of Congress Cataloging-in-Publication Data

Eskapa, Shirley.
  Blood fugue.

  I. Title.
PR6055.S4B56   1986   823'.914   85-28714
ISBN 0-89733-185-0
ISBN 0-89733-205-9 (pbk.)

1

It was the beginning of her second term at the university, and still Ceza Steele had not made, or tried to make, any new friends. During the holidays she'd prepared for the quasi-winter term by acquiring more skirts, blouses and twin-sets. She was wearing the beiges that had been chosen — on the grounds that they best set off her fair colouring — by her parents, Irene and Philip Steele. She still wanted to be a student, for although her grades were uniformly good she was aware, in a kind of dim distress, that she was not; nor could she help knowing that even if she tried to become a real one, it would be irrelevant to her present as well as to her future life. If she made any impression on the others at all it was only that she was indifferent, aloof, residual. She could not overcome this. She was brought to the university by her mother, or by a driver, or by Paul Goodman, then she was fetched at lunchtime, returned and fetched again.

Each morning break she telephoned her mother and Paul.

The telephones were in the foyer of the main block. Ceza could not help reading posters — sometimes they were even tacked onto the walls of the phone booths.

OPEN MINDS IN OPEN UNIVERSITIES
UNIVERSITY INDEPENDENCE VIOLATED
KNOWLEDGE IS COLOURBLIND
FREEDOM IS INDIVISIBLE

Ceza read them, and, reading them, felt there was something improper about them, like wearing black satin in the middle of the morning.

Which is why Ceza had not known she was going to join the march. It was something that had happened with an unfamiliar, and therefore exhilarating spontaneity. And even then, if some of the lecturers had not cancelled their lectures, she doubted whether she would have allowed herself to be a naive outsider in that unreal throng. But, as it was, there she stood, rather cold, on the exonerating island of rough *kikuyu* grass outside the gates of the university. She'd been pushed somewhat to the back of the crowd, and seemed only to stamp her feet (but merely against the cold) with the rest of them. The group was quiet. It was an attentive rhythmic quiet, for they were being addressed by student leaders. Ceza could hear nothing, but looked ahead — bravely — as if she not only heard but was in deep accord with the speaker. The winter sun throbbed against her eyes, so she took out her large heavy sunglasses and behind them felt partly excused and partly forgiving, as if it were both her fault and theirs that she had no idea what the protest was about. It had something to do with medical students, she was sure; there were so many of them about. . . .

Then the crowd was unbalanced, pushed back. Ceza could discern, and even felt part of, self-righteous expressions of protest. The thick precise volley from the engineering students, who had come to break up the meeting, eclipsed the speaker's civilized educated tones. And then suddenly, on someone's shoulders, she saw the student she had so often seen in the foyer when she made her telephone calls, and his voice, neither shouting nor urgent, but controlled with the unhasty throb of reasoned acrimony, bore through and silenced those heckling engineers. "Unjust laws can never be justly defended," rang out. As if at a command, they began their orderly march. It was then the police, with batons consonant with the engineers' interpretation of responsibility, broke up the march. . . . The students had not been granted official permission to protest. And in the pummelling, stampeding disorder that was let loose, Ceza heard, "Indra's been knocked down." But he was up again, on other shoulders, his voice authoritatively ordering them to make their own way to the magistrates' courts. There was a rush to the bus stop. Ceza joined in, and then, outlandishly and quite beyond her intention, held up her hand to thumb a lift. A motorist stopped immediately. "Hold it!" someone yelled, and unbelievably Indra and a medical student jumped into the car. Indra's face was bleeding, and the handkerchief he held against it, though bloodsodden, was distinctly made of Swiss lawn, like Paul's mother's, Ceza noted, more astonished at this than at her own importunity in having become a hitch-hiker.

"We'd be grateful, sir, if you could give us a lift to the magistrates' courts," Indra said.

"That would be very kind of you, sir," Ceza put in.

She had never addressed anyone as "sir" in her life. She found herself offering a new handkerchief, while she did not forget to smile flirtatiously at the driver who said, "No trouble at all. My pleasure. What's all the trouble about anyway?"

Ceza, who did not know, could not reply, and turned, with the utmost delicacy of deference to Indra, indicating his authority.

"Six medical students were arrested for holding a private meeting. During a tea-break at medical school," Indra said.

"What for?" the motorist asked.

"For holding a meeting," Ceza answered. She felt foolish. The motorist looked familiar. Perhaps he worked for her father?

"They want to have the right to work on white cadavers."

"Dead bodies?" the motorist said, sounding knowledgeable.

"Yes. Dead bodies." Indra nailed a laugh, as if even this sound was yet another inevitable transaction with the absurd. "They'd never be as daring as to ask to work on a real living white —" He paused, chuckled again, then added, "Human?" but doubtfully, as if he felt that the only human whites could be dead whites. The motorist caught Ceza's gaze to share the insult at least. Ceza had automatically and in instant sympathy turned towards him. Still shielded by her sunglasses she elected to say, "Isn't it ridiculous? Would a body know the difference between an African student and a white one?"

"And would it matter if it could?" Indra said.

But Ceza's glasses could not conceal a flush that was spreading along her neck.

"Ah, you blush," said Indra. "No, there are not enough white cadavers to go round. You know, like skilled labour, the demand exceeds the supply . . . and in the end we have to fall on the blacks to do the job. More blacks, more black cadavers." And then, but without a

10

hint of insolence, he slipped in, "I'm sure you would agree, sir."

"More readily than you would believe," the motorist said. He seemed to struggle with himself, as if he did not want to say anything more, yet added helplessly, defensively, "Haven't I given you a lift?"

He braked, and a child's tin lorry fell from the windscreen ledge. Struck by the agreeable improbability of the company in the car, Ceza said only, "I see you have a small son."

"Yes," the motorist murmured. Unforthcomingly.

By now it was clear that he was nervous, for his eyes in the rearview mirror darted, behind his shoulders as it were — and when Indra's wound had begun to spurt afresh, the eyes in the mirror reflected less sympathy than distaste.

The white-coated student next to Indra said, "You're spilling onto the upholstery, man."

"It's only my blood," Indra said mildly. "My own blood always surprises me — we're not supposed to have any, are we, sir?" His and the motorist's glances dissected for a moment in the mirror. "Still, we *do* make good cadavers."

The laughter that followed was pitched at the level of trifling titters heard at an exhibition, and the motorist, in the manner of one who is regained by any kind of laughter, said, "Do you mind if I drop you all off at the corner before we get to the courts?"

"Of course not," said Ceza, fever-bright. She was conscious that the motorist did not want to be seen with them, that he was afraid, and she received his fear, unaccountably, she thought, as though it were the promise of a scrap of life.

She turned toward Indra. She had never known herself to make a more meticulously intimate movement: consequently, it was her eyes that slid away.

Once outside the car and shivering on the street-corner Ceza said, "It was nice of him to have given us a lift. . . ?"

Indra's blood was on the handkerchief; it had thickened like cherry jam on a napkin; it had become necessary for him to hold it in place.

Indra turned to the white coat beside him, "Come on — it'll probably be crowded. Mr. Generous drove with excessive caution."

Dismissed, Ceza could do nothing but scurry after them.

In the wide corridor outside Court G, people — the rocking crowd of coloreds, Africans, Indians and a sprinkling of whites — swayed as if by wind instead of their own momentum. The crowd parted when Indra arrived and Ceza was left behind. She called his name once, at which the crowd again parted; undifferentiated eager smiles willed her through. She passed through them, but felt weightless. She felt celebrated and, beyond safety, said thank you, thank you, her voice sounding tongueless. Inside the courtroom the crowds buzzed. There seemed to be no room for Ceza. She approached the spectators' seats, moving unhesitatingly to where the whites were clustered, and a place was made for her. It was then that she saw the brown dividing bar; in her eyes it was like a ballet rail. Her eyes beamed after Indra, sighted and held him in their focus. She saw him see her once, but he gave no sign and only made more notes. Rammed tight on the brown bench that was her seat, she felt too unimportant to be real. All at once a note was handed to her, and though she had never before seen

Indra's handwriting, she knew that it was from him. It said tersely, *"In court women must wear a head-cover."*

Prodigal with delight — he had recognized her femininity — she looked toward him again but he gave no sign of having seen. A recess was announced. Ceza turned to the large African standing beside her, though thoroughly separated by that brown bar.

"Would you mind lending me your scarf?" she said.

"My scarf?"

"I have to cover my head with something."

"Of course you can have my scarf, ma'am," he said. He unwound it from his neck as he spoke. "It's rather long, as you can see —"

"That doesn't matter. I didn't know women had to cover their heads."

"One thing *we* know about is how to appear in court."

"I can imagine that."

He leaned towards her to place the thick blue-grey striped scarf about her shoulders, and she moved towards him to make it easier. Cameras began to click. He turned from her then, to face them full-faced, and Ceza, unaware of the cameras, turned towards them, too. She knew she was being photographed, she also knew she was behind her sunglasses. Still, she covered her face, and, in the flurry of bending her neck — as if listening to a whisper — breathed in the smell that had lodged in the scarf, and understood she had never been so close to an African before — no, not even when she had been rocked to sleep against the nannie Jessica's bountiful breasts. . . . The scarf smelt tantalizingly, Ceza believed, of life: of sweat and fear, but mainly of flesh. The courtroom lost its distinctiveness and its furnishings dwindled from her puffed mind. The raking voices of the police, the crammed

13

breathing, surged and dizzied; her chest stiffened with wonder, like a child at a circus; whenever someone entered the courtroom she heard brief bursts of the abruptly silenced sad melody of the African national anthem. The hush was suddenly broken, and the sharp commonplaceness of a raised voice invading the courtroom from the corridor alerted Ceza's circus-excitement to something of a different edge, into a recognition of the kind of danger that might be finally relevant.

"Margaret, Margaret, don't you talk to me like that!" The voice, debased and ugly, but in the timbre of her own neighbourhood, or of Paul's golf-club, though now a yowl, was heard distinctly as if she'd heard someone crying, "Ceza Steele! Ceza Steele!" It rose in triumphant despair, "We'll take you overseas. *Margaret — Margaret* . . . I'll catch you . . ."

The student whose scarf she wore said, "We didn't introduce ourselves. My name is Thomas Matau."

"Ceza Steele."

"Glad to know you."

"Same here."

"Ugly-sounding scene . . . ?"

"Horrible."

"It was worse than that," he said reprovingly.

"Of course it was," she said quickly, scornfully — establishing at once that it was not her fault.

"If it was worse than horrible — what was it?"

"Disgusting."

"Ah disgusting — only disgusting?"

Flushed, feeling her boundaries invaded, Ceza twisted the scarf.

"Well — if you must hide behind black glasses, how can one know what you think — ?"

14

Ceza removed them at once. "I'd forgotten about them," she lied.

"Tell me," Thomas said politely, "Tell me, what was disgusting. Margaret's affair with one's friend?"

"Uh — you know them?" Ceza interrupted. Too avidly.

"One is curious," Thomas said. "These things happen you know —" And then as if he had read her mind, he answered — "Yes, one has known this sort of thing oneself —"

Ceza refused to flinch.

"I see," she murmured. The sunglasses felt sticky between her fingers. She ached to put them on. She remembered that she was supposed to meet Paul for lunch and glanced as unnoticeably as possible at the large brown clock. She never wore a watch. Yes she had time — she could phone him in about forty-five minutes. She'd cancel. He'd understand. She breathed on the glasses and began to polish them with the borrowed scarf.

"Those glasses aren't lensed," he said. "One can easily see that."

"No," she agreed, regained. "No — they're not. I hope your liaison didn't have the tragic ending we've just heard."

"One knows when things are unendable — when all advice is without point."

She murmured again, "I see."

"No —" he said firmly. "One can see that you have never been in love. One sees that at once — one saw that as soon as the glasses were off . . ."

"You did?" she said questioningly. Yet could not stifle a frank coquettish gleam. "You could be wrong, you know . . ."

15

"Of course. One always knows that. But not this time."

Attempting the light-hearted approach, she said, "You confuse me, you know . . ."

"That was one's intention." He laughed, Ceza thought, promiscuously. She flushed. She could not have believed that she found Thomas, well — enticing — as if he'd beckoned her to some unknowable place.

"One perceives your prettiness, your glamour — you're too fashionable to know anything about love," Thomas said. And with a flimsy movement of his hands he indicated that she was the sort of person whom one gave up without even trying . . .

Her alien's curiosity was exchanged for an alien's bewilderment — Thomas might have been speaking a foreign tongue. At any rate he was showing off, she saw, and not entirely innocent of malice, either. And if he'd wanted to show her how white she was, he'd succeeded . . . She'd have to phone Paul: not to phone him would somehow be too damning. Besides, there had been photographs — what explanation could she give to her parents . . . ? In her mind's eye she saw herself inside the telephone booth, insulated, quite unprickable and well within her preordained environment.

She turned to Thomas. "Excuse me," she said. "I have to make a phone call. I must cancel an arrangement."

"Let him wait."

"I couldn't do that —" Ceza said, and stood up.

"You've been well trained."

"What — ? Yes," she laughed miserably. "It looks like it."

She began to leave, turned towards him to pass, and

16

then remembered about the petty-brown bar that barricaded him from her.

"You forgot?" Thomas said.

"Yes."

"My scarf—?"

"I almost forgot. But I'm coming right back—"

"One can't be sure."

Unwinding it from her head and neck she felt she was coming out of an embrace. She gave it back reluctantly, though with a flourish.

It was hot inside the telephone booth.

Ceza felt over-crowded. The nagging sour smell that came from the mouthpiece irritated her. She'd have to wait, she was told, the doctor was examining—and, scrabbling about in her handbag for more small change she felt, in a dispersed and congested way—messy. She imaginged Paul, immaculate, cool, and blamed him. Besides if he didn't come quickly she'd have to hang up; she ought to have had more change. Consequently, when she heard his voice, she snapped, "I'm in a call-box. 243725. You'll have to call back." She let out her breath. "243725."

She'd cut across his "Dr. Goodman, here." This was characteristic enough to have alerted him. He said, "You're hyperventilating. What's the matter?"

"I'm not at 'varsity'," she cried, triumphant. "This is a different call-box."

"Well, where are you?"

"Near the magistrates' courts."

"Good God," he said, she thought, scathingly. "What on earth are you doing there?"

"I need to go back. I won't be able to meet you for lunch."

"I think you should tell me what's going on, don't you? Don't you think you should?"

"I'm sorry," she said. "I thought I had."

Appeased, he said, "No you haven't." He added affectionately, "Funnyface —"

She hesitated. She said, "I went to a protest meeting. Then we all landed up at the courts."

"Who?"

"People in my class."

"Which class?"

"African administration." She floundered. Her voice hit a note of certainty. "You remember, the syllabus your Whyte fitted into."

"So you want to put me off?"

"It's not that."

"But that's what you're doing." His voice chilled her. "I wouldn't do that to you. It's Friday. I've booked our table."

Her limp energy left her. "Yes," she said, and sounded ashamed.

"I'll fetch you? Where are you?"

"I don't know the name of the street I'm in. It'll be better if I meet you there —"

"Fine."

She thought: "There's a patient sitting in front of him — listening to all this." She said: "Do you love me?"

"Of course." He spoke warmly, and his voice struck her with its incorrigible efficiency. Medical tenderness.

Ceza did not want to meet him. She was aware that she was an untidy blur of disappointment and tired, tired — illogically tired, as if she watched herself asleep. And

18

only a little earlier when she'd been under the shelter of that greasy scarf she'd felt undamageable, noble, tangibly courageous even . . . No matter how bewildered or alien, no matter how helpless . . .

And so Ceza told Paul all about the protest, the motorist, the court, the photographers — even the scarf.

"But *darling,* this is not you at all."

"Oh," she said emptily. "Well, what are we going to do?"

"I know some of the editors," he said.

"Oh," her voice wriggled like the fork against her plate. "Do you?"

"Funnyface, you *know* I do —"

"I'd forgotten —"

"Well, you're upset. You've hardly touched your food." He smiled then. "See how you need me to look after you —"

"Yes."

"I'll simply stop the publication of those photographs. Mind you, it won't be too easy — leave it to me. I'll tell them who you are. Hell, your father advertises in them every day —"

"That should not make any difference," she interrupted, sounding almost confident, at last.

Emphatically scornful, he said, "I don't know what's got into you, but whatever it is, it's not going to do you or anyone any good."

"How," she asked as if she could not be expected to understand, "could this harm you?"

More than somewhat disconcerted by her unretreating eyes he looked at her suspiciously, checkingly. "But you *must* know . . . Of course you *do* know."

"It's true I don't photograph well —"

"*Ceza.*"

Was this a quarrel? She couldn't be sure. Up until now it had seemed that quarrels, like chess or bridge, were something they did not go in for: and if they actually were arguing it was astonishingly less emptying than the arabesques of conciliation. It was a fresh experience, startling, so new that it was like something no one could explain. She said, "I'm unphotogenic."

"Now you *know* you're being silly," he said patiently. "You're very photogenic."

She felt unendurably sly, yet knew that she could not have done otherwise: she had risen above herself. She said, "Have you had your nose done?"

"Who told you?" Paul asked in a voice that tried not to go too far.

"So it's true. Well it's beautiful anyway," she said quickly. "It's made you perfect. It really has —"

"I suppose I should have told you. It didn't occur to me. I've got so used to it."

"You won't be mad with me, will you?" Ceza said as if this was all that mattered.

Caught by her interminable stare he said sadly, "I love you —"

By way of an answer she grasped his endless hands and carried them to her lips.

At last he said, "Let's go —"

"To the flat?"

"Yes," he said, standing up. Impatient for the bill.

"But you're expected at the rooms —"

"I'll tell them I had to deal with an emergency. It'll be true, too —" He dropped some notes on the plate. "We'll have at least twenty minutes, if we hurry —"

Ceza had not moved. She stood up now, heavily,

20

tentative, as if her brain (which also felt swollen) teetered on its perch of exhaustion. She wanted to race there with him, but her tiredness interceded and she not only wanted, but felt she ought to want . . .

Paul had taken the little flat soon after Ceza and he had, as they put it, got together. It was close to the university and not too far from his rooms. Paul lived with his parents, as was only proper. This flat was their secret. It was as temporary as it was convenient. And very different from Villa Evermor, the house her parents had bought thirteen years ago, when she was the sweet and serious six-year-old her parents still saw, no matter which way they looked at her. The Steeles lived in one of those suburbs, about a twenty-minute drive from Johannesburg's centre, which people spoke of as "being out at Uvongo," as if all those mansions — intercoms, sauna baths, burglar alarm-sirens notwithstanding — were no more ordinary bungalows of the veld. So it was the very tastelessness of both buildings and furnishings that Ceza found appealing and even exciting. And yet, even after her clamouring nerves had been dealt with, she felt an uneasiness too close to the kind of discontent she believed she had no right to feel. She thought of Thomas's scarf, of its smell and the flat seemed sterile and as artificial as Paul's nose.

Unaccountably, and quite without believing she meant to, she said, "I often wonder about Whyte —"

He stirred lazily. "What did you say?"

"If it hadn't been for Whyte, you and I . . . Well, the night of the funeral, you know —"

"What are you talking about?"

"It was death that brought us together."

She appeared withdrawn, moody, almost indifferent. His instant diagnosis of what he saw as her uncharacteristic behaviour was that she had become "hostile" to him. No matter—he would compel her interest. He said, "What happened to Whyte was in a sense—at least to me—even more profound than death. Does that sound strange to you?" He went on slowly. "I behaved unethically, betrayed my profession. I could be struck off the rolls, you know—I wasn't looking after him. It was not a case of a doctor failing his patient. Misdiagnosis is not dishonest—" His hands made a bewildered movement. "I falsified his death certificate. Is that enough for you?"

Ceza knew she must listen, and with fanatic attention; she strained after every syllable. An understanding of all that she had not known came to her as easily as the events she and Paul had shared. For although Ceza and Whyte had never met, she had travelled hundreds of miles to go to his funeral.

Certainly Sarah Goodman, Paul's mother, believed that Whyte's death had brought Ceza into her son's life. Though the real shock was the way in which a servant—a dead servant—had become so remorselessly important to her. But then the whole thing had been illogical from the start. Indeed, Sarah frequently thought that the very senselessness of it all ought to have been enough to have cancelled its truth: what was senseless could not also be real. She would review the events which had, she believed, compelled her to test her pie. What would have happened, she wondered, if she had given Whyte only one slice instead of the entire remains of the same pie that had all but killed her sister and brother-in-law?

There had been no warning. The week had begun ordinarily enough. It had been her habit (no more than fitting for the wife of Advocate Louis Goodman) to plot out the week's activities. She did this at her bedroom desk because it was private, and because she liked its pale pinks and frilled lace lamp-shades. It was only since their house had been sold that each hour of the day had to be accounted for. The Goodmans and their only child Paul had lived in one of those old Johannesburg houses of Parktown, or, as Sarah would have put it — in one of those distinguished old Parktown homes — a Sir Herbert Baker house, built in the nineteen-twenties. Sarah always smiled when she talked of that house — with that gentle smile she did not know she reserved for the tenderly remembered dead. They had left the house five years ago and although the garden still bloomed, and the house thrived with a young family, it had as much life for Sarah, who often passed it, as the cement-coloured tombstone of her mother's grave. Yet she grieved for that house — for its cool spaces, its massive beamed living-room with its giant untidy fireplace, for its trees gone anatomical with age.

And now she was confronted with this flat, shapeless, undistinguished — flat — too geometric, too pale to accommodate their outsize stink-wood dining-room suite, which Sarah regarded as majestic. Now they had only left-overs, and the breakfast-room suite now served as the dining-room, and the spare-room suite engulfed the marital room. Still, it was a comfortable flat — she could not deny that — it had two bathrooms, and Louis still had his study . . . And now that those terrible days of the share swindle seemed extinct — and they could well afford it — what would be the point of buying another

23

house with Paul grown up? He was a doctor, and entitled to a life of his own, as Sarah agreed — besides his bedroom was the largest in the flat — Sarah had done it up as a study. It was a successful room, left-over furniture notwithstanding.

You could do a lot with left-overs, if you tried hard enough, and made the best of what you had. Look at Whyte, the cook, who unlike her old Jeremiah (of fifteen years service) had not refused to come with them to the flat, even though he had to live in a cell-like room on the top floor, in one of those "locations in the sky" where women visitors were forbidden, and, for that matter, men, too. Sometimes, Sarah thought with an illicit half-shamed smile (who would believe that she could think like this?) Whyte was the most meaningful of all the left-overs of the old house, even more meaningful than the desk she sat at, and the desk was at least three hundred years old. It was almost as if Whyte were a part of her most secret inner life: with his little immaculate beard tacked to his polished black face he had, for Sarah, a ridiculous sense of class (he claimed that he was descended from an old chief or something like that). He enjoyed a unique sense of dignity and disdain peculiar to the domestic-snob. Sarah had noticed that her own sister, Doris, seemed uncomfortable with him — uncomfortable enough to ask after his health. In the old house his fierce rule of his subordinates had gone, as if by attachment to his fiercer loyalty to Sarah and woe betide a servant who drank from a family glass or who forgot to cut the crusts from the bread — (you never knew who or what might have touched the bread — oh, he was well-trained). Like all good officers, Whyte set a good example, and so enhanced his prestige. He would not so much as touch left-over food without his mistress's permission. Only anger relieved his sullen grim dealings with his fellow servants — now only a wash-girl and a flat-boy who came in every day. With Louis Goodman he was the soul of obsequiousness.

Sarah really believed that she trusted Whyte (the deep-freeze keys were in his keeping) yet when a telegram had come from a distant village informing Whyte of his father's death, Sarah first asked to see the telegram before she gave him the necessary written permission to return home for the funeral. She offered no sympathy. He expected none. "You are a very good madam," he said, when she granted him leave.

Prudence had constrained Sarah to denigrate Whyte whenever the endemic South African servant-problem cropped up in company. "No one but me would put up with him," she would sigh. "I should let him go — but you know me—" at this moment she usually paused and smiled weakly— "I haven't the heart to get rid of him. I have to close my ears to all his cheek." But lately, protected by new statutes, Sarah altered her habitual comment. She now offered that it was "terribly hard to get good servants these days," and that "Whyte would have to do." Whyte had been born in a distant African village and under the new law was permitted to work only for Sarah. If he left her employ, he would be forced to return to his small village where there was no work and much soil erosion. Whyte, like her diamonds or her motor car, belonged to her. Whyte was irrevocably in her name. To pay a servant as little as possible was clever — the ultimate art as far as Sarah was concerned. But she had always been good to Whyte. His children wore Paul's old clothes in their distant village and she did not make him pay.

"None of them appreciate anything you do for them," was Sarah's maxim, so that whatever she did for Whyte was the result of a lost battle with her principles.

She found safety in suffering: "Life is hard, Whyte." Whyte always nodded in sympathetic and sad agreement, "Yes, Madam. I know, Madam. Terrible."

"They all let you down, you only get kicks for thanks," it was like an amen at the end of almost every conversation. Her sadness mystified Whyte: "Madam was well-treated by Master, Master was rich, Paul was a doctor, the servants gave no trouble." She had all of Whyte's perplexed pity just as she had all of his loyalty. It was her eyes he pitied . . . those eyes which were clamped in a permanent reproach, as if she had been born reproaching the whole world. Whyte had never known why the house had been sold. Perhaps — Sarah wondered now — she should have told him?

She left her desk and crossed to the kitchen whose sight was sure of solace. The kitchen breathed asepsis and functionalism. Chrome handles ornamented the nullish cream of the walls and the cupboards, the way coffin handles can invoke the look of living furniture. The yellow hanging plastic strips intransigently stained with the death-struggles of flies, like all the impedimenta of the kitchen, suffered a daily washing. Bone-white muslin curtains, heavy with starch, feebly tackled the fan-produced breeze. All the sugars and spices, coffees and pickles failed to cleanse the cheerless air of disinfectants, deodorants and detergents. Insects terrified Sarah. Together with Whyte and her much-trusted oven (both the oven and Whyte had never let her down), Sarah produced excellent results. Duty-bound to outwit the recipe books, she concocted intricate blends of essences as a substitute

26

for Jamaican rum or other expensive ingredients and her dishes were imaginative and unfathomably delicious.

However, Sarah regarded cooking like looking after the family as but a job to be done. She lived her life like some kind of ponderous secret — yet was dismayed by the gap in her weekly diary — nothing to do on Thursday... She fidgeted her lips and tucked them into her mouth — boredom was akin to grief. She would phone Doris, she and Doris could always organize something. She went back to her bedroom — it was more private to phone from there. Doris's phone was engaged — it would be hopeless trying to arrange canasta on a Thursday afternoon when everyone's cook was off. She tried again — still engaged. Who was Doris talking to for so long? The telephone was indispensable to the sisters, as if it were a vital extra limb without which all activity would cease. Solicitous of puce nail varnish, they dialled one another several times daily.

The sisters remarked often upon their closeness and gloried in it. We are very close — we are so close — yes, we are very close and "blood, of course, is thicker than water" they would say over and over again to one another more as though they believed *in* what they said rather than in what *was* said. Many thousands of phone calls had been and many more were still to be, before the sisters were to realize that they were, in truth, as close to one another as to the butcher, to whom for years and years they had both telephoned their orders... Sarah never told Doris the true reason for selling her house — and if Doris had suspected anything, shouldn't Sarah at least be spared?

Doris's phone was still engaged. Sarah glanced at the large masculine clock which she resented as much as the rush of time. A grateful client of Louis's (an electrical manufacturer) had presented him with a numberless clock: the twelve letters of her husband's name — Louis Goodman — told the time. The clock bore a small engraved plaque: "TO THE GREATEST ADVOCATE WITH THE GREATEST SENSE OF TIMING." It did not go with the pinks, and ought to be in the study, Sarah told herself with the petulant helplessness of a permanent reproach — but Louis insisted. It was half-past ten, and Doris must have been out of her bath for at least half an hour, Sarah calculated, and so it couldn't be a servant on the phone.

"Who've you been talking to?" Sarah asked irritably.

"I wasn't on the phone long," the other said defensively.

"I've been trying for thirty minutes — at *least* thirty minutes."

They arranged, after forty minutes or so, that Doris would get an appointment for Thursday afternoon.

Canasta, the telephone, a French conversation class and the anticipation dispatched (and sweetened) the three days before the dressmaker's appointment that Doris had arranged. Sarah liked collecting the names of women who dressed cheaply, but who passed themselves off as habituées of the expensive shops.

At the dressmaker's they discussed styles, prices, materials and her other customers. The visit was more profitable than Sarah's highest expectations — so profitable that Doris, who had dropped Sarah home automatically, stopped at Sarah's for a cup of tea, and forgot that it was Thursday and that her cook was off . . .

"You know, I still can't get over it," Sarah repeated, as Whyte, without having had to be asked, brought the tea-tray.

28

"Irene Steele . . ." Doris loitered over the words, "well you live and learn . . . They've been very rich people for twenty years . . ."

"At least twenty."

Doris adjusted a giggle. "More money — more pig — as they say," she said. (Because Doris's husband was a millionaire, not by design, but by chance, Doris and Sarah felt justified in scouring the supermarkets for sardines sold at the cheapest price, and to patronise cheap dressmakers.)

Sarah said, "She's very reasonable — you can't say she isn't."

"No, you can't," Doris agreed. "Who says she isn't?"

"I was just saying," Sarah said.

Doris had another cup of tea, they talked of Paul, who at twenty-three was still refusing to specialize. The sound of Whyte latching the curtains drew Doris to her watch. "Oh, my God! It's so late — I didn't realize — and the girl's off to-day — I forgot."

"What are you making?" Sarah asked.

"I was going to pop into Crystal's and buy some cold meats. But they'll be closed now. And all the meat's in the freezer . . ."

"Really, Doris . . ." Sarah said reprovingly. "Who buys cold meats? It's dangerous, honestly it is . . ."

Doris, at not time unaffected by her older sister's reproach, said nervously, "If your husband likes them — what can you do?"

"Don't be upset," Sarah said calmingly, indulging a solicitude that was not entirely undidactic. "Come into the kitchen . . . he'll have a wonderful supper. You'll have nothing to worry about!"

Before Sarah unlocked the deep-freeze door she slightly

fondled its cool curve. She dawdled her purple nail down a list sellotaped to the inside of the door. The list specified the frozen item, its shelf, its position on the shelf, and the date it had been frozen. Whyte had long since appropriated those secretarial duties. (Actually, Sarah knew the precise location of what she seemed to be looking for — a chicken-mushroom pie — but she was always trying to teach Doris to be more efficient.) The pie was wrapped in tin-foil, and sealed in polythene. "You know my chicken-mushroom pie," she said smilingly, and then detailed the oven instructions which then she repeated. "And take this salad, too — you can always give me back the bowl, and Whyte will quickly make another one. It's no trouble to you eh, Whyte?"

"No, Madam," Whyte said (but sullenly, Doris felt).

"The children are on holiday," Doris excused weakly. "Thanks, Sarah. Thanks a million."

"We had a good afternoon," Sarah said, as she accompanied her to the car. "But do me a favour, listen to me: don't buy ready-made cooked food. You never know . . ."

Doris and her husband's rush to the bathroom began five hours later. Doris managed to telephone the doctor before losing consciousness. The doctor lost valuable time in rousing the servants to let him in — (they thought it was a police raid and would not answer) — but lost no time at all in diagnosis and treatment. The next morning, weak though she was — she felt as though her very intestines had been washed away — Doris phoned Sarah from the hospital to tell her what had happened. Sarah did not believe her — "Don't worry, I'm coming at once. When are they discharging you?" She didn't wait for an answer but said, "Don't worry, I'll come and fetch you."

Sarah dressed rapidly. It was absurd, she thought, to blame her chicken-mushroom pie. After all, who else sterilized everything in the kitchen? Cut the crusts of bread? Tested every tin? She was the victim of slander, that's what she was. She stopped at Doris's house to find out what cold meats they had eaten — no cold meats, only the pie and the salad. Couldn't be the salad — Doris had distinctly mentioned something about mushrooms ... She sniffed the left-over pie — it smelt delicious. Satisfied, she wrapped it carefully, and put it in the boot of her car. Later, she brought the unharmed but weakened Goodmans home.

That night Sarah asked Whyte to stay in. He often helped Sarah bake at night, usually when a cake was needed for a fête. With the evolved ease of a twenty-year association, Whyte listened while Sarah talked. At the end of such an engagement, Whyte made Sarah tea and, usually, whilst he set the tea-tray, Sarah selected something for him to eat in his room. Tonight she gave him some chicken-mushroom pie.

As much a creature of routine as his mistress, Whyte never shared his bounty. Long ago Sarah had asked him not to — "the other servants will also expect," — and Whyte had cherished his privilege. It was late when he reached his cell-sized cement-floored room and he was hungry and weary. He preferred to eat with his hand. Whyte undressed slowly and, clothed in Louis Goodman's faded monogrammed pyjamas, he went to bed. Very slowly, in his brick-raised high bed, under a brilliantly embroidered white calico coverlet, Whyte ate the chicken-mushroom pie.

Co-ordinated, turbulent vomiting and diarrhoea hurled Whyte awake. His body shook in gigantic spasms. When he was not vomiting, he tried to call for help. With the superhuman strength unique to matters of survival, Whyte instinctively fought his way to the door. The terrifying sight of two doors instead of one sent him crashing to the highly polished concrete floor. His brief thought of his drought-ridden Kraal drowned in his desperate thirst.

The next morning, when their early-morning tea did not arrive, Sarah sent the flat-boy (who was cleaning windows) upstairs, to investigate. Other servants helped him smash Whyte's complicated locks. The flat-boy's screams woke Paul, and the three Goodmans followed him to Whyte's room. Halfburied in its own excrement Whyte's body lay in the abandon of a drunken sprawl . . .

Paul's medical bag felt heavy with uselessness. "He's dead," he said, and added diagnosingly, "smells like botulism poisoning . . ." He looked toward Whyte's tin plate, which, but for a few pastry flakes, was empty.

Sarah echoed his gaze. In a held-in hush of fear she whispered, "I feel very ill . . . very bad."

"Come — we'll take you home," Paul said.

Hunched forward, then bent double, Sarah allowed them to help her to her flat. Her high-heeled backless slippers flapped, and shortened her step across the servant's mean pimply-walled passage. Her hair was piled high under its sleep-net. She clutched the folds of her scarlet dressing-gown as if she were protecting both the gown and her stomach from falling apart. She moaned briefly, carnally, as if her suddenly overburdened viscera had concertinaed downward under the strain of her shock. Incredulity was heavier than grief. "I can't understand it . . . I can't understand it . . ." she kept whimpering.

"We'll understand more after the post-mortem," Paul said.

"Post-mortem?" Sarah repeated raspingly.

"Of course there's always a post-mortem in a case like this."

"Oh, no — we can't have one," Sarah whispered. "I gave him the pie."

"That needn't have caused it. What sort of pie?"

"A chicken-mushroom pie." Sarah looked nervously at her husband who had got up to shut the door.

"Mushrooms could well be the culprit," Paul said in the therapeutically speculative accents of his profession. "Post-mortems eliminate guess-work."

"No," Sarah moaned, "no-no-no-no-no . . ."

"Stop that, Sarah," her husband said sternly. "We're in enough trouble as it is."

Sarah's moaning shrivelled to a whimper.

"Paul — you'll sign the death certificate?" he said as if he were presenting a statement to the court.

"I can't do that . . ."

"But we're *asking* you to," Sarah said reproachfully. "You've got to . . . What have I ever asked of you . . . only that you study . . . always kicks for thanks . . . Do I have to beg my own flesh and blood?"

Her reproach unerringly pierced Paul, and stayed with him, until he felt threatened by it. He listened to his father explain in the devitalized tones of legal logic, about Doris and then conclude: "Well — if you won't do it — I know a dozen doctors who will!"

Sarah rocked mechanically. "My own flesh and blood . . . my own . . ."

"Clearly you're not asking so much of your own flesh

and blood," her husband adeptly inserted. "Now that you understand, Paul, what could be simpler than specifying a coronary thrombosis? Besides — who makes problems over a native servant? A Bantu?"

"Why didn't you tell me . . . ? You had only to tell me . . ." Paul's hands made a bewildered wheedling movement, which, with a sudden flutter, revived his childhood habit. "You'll see that he has a good funeral?" He resigned himself. He said, "You'll go to his funeral of course."

They sighed as we all sigh at a delivery of reason.

Paul telephoned Dr. Jacobs and said that there had been a family crisis, and that he would not be able to do his rounds. His father was anxious that not a word of what had happened should ever become public, and that all the formalities connected with Whyte's disposal should be dealt with quickly and thoroughly. He accordingly announced that he would appear neither at his chambers nor at court.

As soon as these preliminaries were in hand, Advocate Goodman suggested that his wife be given a strong sedative. "You'd better knock her out, Paul," he said.

Sarah wept bitterly, for herself — but wasted no tears on Whyte's dependants whom she had never even seen, whose names she had never known, whose existence (in so far as they had actually had an existence) sprung only from their nuisance potential. When Paul swabbed her arm, she didn't seem any longer to regard him with the proud eyes of maternity, but with the unknowing eyes of a patient in distress. Just before she fell asleep she thought how much easier, just and worthwhile her entire life would have been if only she had had a daughter. She believed she would never forgive Paul for having made

34

her beg him not to go through with an official post-mortem. Meanwhile the advocate had discreetly sent the maid Jacobina to fetch Whyte's pass. It was known legally as a reference book; but it contained no reference however to Whyte's wife, nothing about where she lived, nothing about his children. He then telephoned a firm of undertakers who specialized in African funerals. Africans usually preferred to be buried in earth close to where their families lived, out in the hot dry country, close to farms which Louis Goodman thought of as dumps of sweltering dust. While he waited to be put through to the director of Birds Undertakers (Pty) Ltd he passed Whyte's reference book, rather, its cover, between his fingers. The manufacturers of the plastic cover were clients of his; they'd won the government order with difficulty, had courageously converted their factory from leather to plastics to achieve it, and had, in almost no time at all, Louis Goodman thought ruefully, become one of the largest plastic manufacturers; large enough, in fact, to have given him that clock which told the time in his own name . . . When at last he was put through to the director he said, "Advocate Goodman here. Good morning. An old retainer of ours has unfortunately passed away. Name of Whyte —" he checked the reference book for the surname — "Matambu. Now I understand you handle the usual long distance funerals . . . Good . . . Well, the body will have to be transported a hundred and fifty miles away, or something of that order . . . No problem. Good . . . No, we shall want a better coffin than that . . . No, no need for me to see a catalogue . . . Ornate brass handles and teak . . . That sounds suitable . . . Of course I expect to bear all expense. A loyal and faithful servant of twenty years . . . Indeed, they *are* hard to find.

35

A deposit? Certainly. I'll let your man have it as soon as he comes to collect the body . . . Within the hour? Excellent." He'd adopted his court voice, the one that jarred people into deferential activity. He flicked through the telephone directory; the yellow pages yielded the information he needed. He studied the relevant page with nothing more or less than the same sort of intellectual curiosity he would have awarded a legal treatise, made a decision, then telephoned once more. He spoke to the managing director naturally and, over-riding all mention of impossibility, set the appointment for noon. There was nothing else for it — Whyte's room had to be fumigated and the sooner the better. He lit a cigar. Then he rang the bell above his desk.

Sarah looked at Paul's medical bag which lay open as though empty at the foot of the bed. She had had that bag especially designed — telling him that one day it would be for his grandchildren. Blessing his medical training — for the first and consequently the one exhilarating time — Paul gave her the injection. She slept but even in her sleep her hold on his hand did not unclench — and though his muscles felt cramped, and his bones bruised, he remained stiffly bent over the bed. He would tell her that he would travel to Whyte's funeral. He would be firm about not allowing her to go without him and, this way he would not have let her down.

But once in his room he understood his strategy was too obvious to be effective. Something more was needed — but what? He probed for the weakest point as if he were coaxing an abdomen for the right diagnosis. The answer was obvious. Curiosity! His mother's unconquerable curiosity! Now Sarah would not resist — not if he

36

told her he had invited a girl — say — Ceza Steele — to Whyte's funeral . . . As for himself, a stranger would dilute things — besides, they would have to spend the night at Zandra.

2

Philip Steele did not go to his office on the Saturday morning of Whyte's funeral. He had given his permission for Ceza to accompany the Goodmans with reluctance; the mere request had left him feeling somewhat deprived. His and Ceza's understanding, their good understanding protected them both, he was sure. Still, he had lectured her on trust. She was to keep herself for her husband, that mythical being who had featured in Ceza's life since she was able to think and who had since then asserted the heavy Victorian demands she had never thought to resist. And Irene had prevailed upon him. Because the art of letting a child think she was quite free was when her attachment was forged in knots of blood. And, if you weighted that knowledge with trust — well then . . . Irene talked to him; rather, negotiated, while he emptied his pockets — he had never trusted the final locking up of his head-branch to anyone but himself — not even his deep interest in what she had to say could distract him from his keys.

When Irene was certain that Philip had been convinced that he had decided on Ceza's going she said tranquilly, "Naturally I told Mrs. Goodman that I'd have to speak to you about this. I said I'd phone when you came home."

"She phoned? Sarah Goodman phoned?"

"Of course not. Paul phoned and asked to speak to me. But then his mother was on the phone in no time at all." She hesitated. "I think it would be better if you spoke to them."

"No. I wouldn't think of it. That's *your* department."

As Irene knew.

That the Goodmans were going to travel more than a hundred and fifty miles for the funeral of an old servant, and in this heat, Philip did not question. He doubted whether he would have done the same thing himself, but then he was not a professional man . . .

He was on hand to receive the Goodmans when they swept up his driveway. Paul went into the house to fetch Ceza, and Philip did not invite them in, but chatted in the driveway. He usually spent his summer weekends at home in an old pair of khaki shorts: he liked to show off his muscular chest and didn't give a damn about the gall bladder scar. But Irene had exacted compromise in the form of a shirt and tie — flannels instead of shorts.

Philip said, "Would you mind seeing to it that Ceza phones us when you arrive in Zandra. It's a long journey, you know. Her mother is bound to worry."

"Well now, of course. You can depend on us, sir," Louis said astutely. "Please assure your wife, and be assured yourself that we'll take good care of — uh — your daughter."

"Ceza —" Philip said in a clean, off-key voice.

"Of course — Ceza! Well now, what an interesting name!" Then, shocked though unable to stop, he said, "I come to bury Caesar not to praise him!" He flourished an arm and his tiger's eye cuff links flashed in the sun.

Philip said, "I must say that I think it very nice of you to travel all this way for a servant's funeral. Remarkable."

"It was the very least we could do," Sarah sighed with a self-abolishing smile. "He was more like a member of the family." She sighed thoroughly and resonantly.

Ceza was not especially self-conscious about being with the Goodmans. It had been a week of so many new experiences that *this* part of the excursion seemed only mildly interesting. But then she had not trusted herself to think of what lay ahead — it was as if she was keeping these speculations secret from herself, too . . . Paul turned up the radio — Frank Sinatra's voice spiralled obligingly until Sarah said, "Paul, could you turn that down? We can hardly hear ourselves think. *Quelle tristesse!*"

Paul drove fast and neatly. It was hot and their clothes stuck to the seats. Sarah passed around some lavender water which, in the unity of a heat-daze, they all accepted. The bottled freshness soon evaporated. The air-conditioning had failed. They rolled the windows down and let in more heat instead of air and then they rolled them up again — any breeze disturbed Sarah. Ceza longed to take off the stockings that had become glued to her legs. The lavender water and the heat, and Sarah's pained reaction to both reminded Ceza of being in synagogue upstairs with the ladies on the Day of Atonement, when scent and handkerchiefs came into more play than the prayer books behind which muted conversations were held.

Mr. Shearer, the owner of the Natal Royal Arms Hotel, was waiting on the verandah to greet them. It was the sort of half-sleazy building that used pale pink bougainvillea the way some women might use nail varnish to conceal. But a shingled roof gave off the scent of England that is so especially assumed in that part of Africa, much in the way the Russian upper classes once espoused French. Tea was waiting. They took it in the exactingly shabby chintz and copper lounge. There was time for a quick wash before Mr. Shearer was to lead them to the African cemetery, which was included in the service laid on by Birds Undertakers (Pty) Ltd.

A tall Zulu wearing spectacles and an up-to-date suit stopped them at the cemetery gates. He introduced himself as Oliver Ghashli Matambu, brother of the deceased. He was in the back of the car before they had realized what he was about to do, just as they shook his proffered hand in advance of thought. Sarah sniffed and rolled down the window, it seemed, will-lessly. Far from self-effacing, he was officious and quickly told them that he was in business, had an enterprise of his own, the only member of the family who had not, as he said, "migrated to the big city." The car travelled over the bumpy greyish clay so that "you white people need not walk too far." Suddenly he told them to stop. Now they began to walk over graves that squashed together to save space. Ceza had never trodden on the dead before, the dead are too distant from death to matter. Ceza could not help thinking that the bricks that surrounded the flower beds at the Royal Arms were neater than those edging these graves: things in service matter more, she thought. Soon they had to tread more carefully, so as not to miss their footing and fall into four waiting holes. The place was now more crowded and Ceza was aware of another funeral just ending. Indeed, the priest stood before them apologizing for not having been on hand to greet them; Saturdays were hectic. His apologies covered him as completely as his overworked cassock. Then Ceza was aware of being stared at, of being wondered at, as if they were a bridal party and she the bride.

Sarah's expression was altogether bedraggled. She'd clasped her eyes, whether in supplication or disgust, Ceza could not say—distaste nagged her mouth; her constant nose-blowing sounded like a complaint. A few low ululations, like titters, were let loose, and the priest frowned anxiously and shushed the mourners with his hands, and apologized yet again. Whyte's brother led them to the head of the grave. He walked importantly and Ceza loathed herself for thinking he was showing off the ease with which he handled his visitors. He was like a headmaster welcoming honoured guests to the rostrum on speech day, for his expression was suitably grave and his stride was perfectly sized to dignified expectancy. Whyte's wives were kept to one side—their brother-in-law pointed them out. The coffin waited: shimmering in the sun it seemed to Ceza to be fantastically out of place; the excessive brass handles reminded her of the illicit brandy that Jonas drank that she was not supposed to know about. The priest's Bible was worn and much thumbed—like his cassock it had gone green with age. The service was read, partly in English and partly in Zulu. When the coffin was finally lowered Whyte's brother changed his spectacles to sunglasses. The service ended. And then there was a shuffling, a concerted movement, as something was being carried to the grave. It was an ox hide, red, with a few hairs, as if this hide were old, too. And now Whyte's brother and some other men entered the grave and wrapped it about the coffin. Now more than apologetic the priest was openly ashamed. "Some people will not change their primitive attitudes," he said. But another funeral was waiting. Saturdays, weekends were his busiest time. People still wanted to be buried "at home."

Then the mourners sang, and their song was neither joy nor sorrow, as if death is itself none of these things, neither end nor beginning.

The carpet felt sticky underfoot, and Ceza was obliged to wear the new velvet slippers that Irene had hastily bought. Slippers were enough to have made everything different for Ceza. No one in the Steele household wore them. If the room had held a chair she would have curled up in one — she was reluctant to get between the sheets. She tried sitting on the edge of the bed but the mattress felt spiky as if it had been edged in some sort of hard corrugated cardboard. Besides the blanket felt itchy, surging to her thighs even through the fabric of her chaste Viyella dressing gown and tailored, though, pink pyjamas. She fingered the linen of the pillows and found it surprisingly soft. She was moved to smell the sheets, as if she thought the softness of the linen to be fraudulent. The sheets smelt of the sun and the earth, and Ceza knew they had never been washed in a machine, but outside in the hotel yard.

Paul locked the door behind him.

She never knew how their nightclothes came off.

He was in need of comfort, she'd decided, but what was now happening had only been vaguely dreaded, only vaguely expected, as though it belonged to that nebulous future she had not really believed she'd reach, and had, so to speak, permanently postponed. Even the slight pain she felt had the sensation of reality deferred — there was so much less of it than had been promised. Disbelief overrode every thought, every movement; it was as if she were no more than an irrelevant onlooker at someone else's fantasy. It could all be verified, she knew, but only if she were able to share the experience with a third person.

Paul mistook her detachment for submissiveness, and told her that he knew things had not been too successful for her, but that she'd been brave, and things would improve, he'd make her happy. He said he loved her, and, though he hated the idea, he thought it prudent to return to his own room.

Ceza was awakened by sharp raps against the door. A slight and shy and very shiny African maid who called Ceza "Missus" though she was about the same age, brought her some tea. It was too milky, but she drank it gratefully. She was hungry, which conferred a sense of time — but not acceptance — upon her.

She did not want to be late and was at the breakfast table before the others.

She studied the dining-room carefully, as if attempting to locate herself spatially, at least . . . She'd never stayed at such a hotel, and this was her first visit to a country town. It was a grimy place, paint peeled, the same banana skin shades, but the tableclothes were as white, with the same hushing whiteness, as the sheets had been. No, she wouldn't order yet, she said looking around the empty room. She was waiting. Yes, it was true, she had come down for a funeral, even though she had never even seen the man who had died. I am sure you have a lot of people staying at your hotel, she said, for the manager was becoming indignant, and of course there's

45

no accounting for human tastes. She herself couldn't understand how an advocate of the importance of Louis Goodman could have taken so much trouble. She didn't know him well. Yes, she knew the son better, but, no, she hadn't known him very long. Really, you saw him walking down the corridor at about half-past five in the morning? Perhaps his mother had been ill? Paul was a doctor. Oh yes, qualified for two years or eighteen months.

She tried to look beyond the room, through the windows, but they were a screen of dust. On her side, though, a few whining flies busied themselves, hovering one above the other. Were they mating? She couldn't be sure. She supposed that she'd had a marriage night. At least technically. And if so this was her wedding breakfast. A technicality instead of a feeling.

Anyway . . .

Ceza felt odd, almost improper, sitting alone in the dining-room, then remembered she had always been with her mother whenever they'd gone to the restaurant floor of one of the big departmental stores.

She brightened precisely. She could tell her mother about this, at least, she thought. As for the other, it hadn't happened. She suspected that she might have grown up, but felt no elation. Perhaps this was adulthood? But adulthood was like worry, was something her father had assured her she'd never have to deal with, not even after he was dead. Perhaps she'd sinned? But she could manage nothing more than a feeling of transgression at sitting alone in a large and shapelessly distant dining-room. She recounted the Ten Commandments, but could not find herself guilty. She thought she ought to be timid at the thought of seeing Paul again, but was not. She felt nothing, only the imperative to be polite, to be on her best behaviour, so as not to let her parents down.

Breakfast was large and plentiful, but Ceza only asked for pawpaw. All the Goodmans had bacon, shocking Ceza exquisitely. She'd never even sat at the same table as bacon before! And Louis Goodman — a dignitary on the board of the synagogue. At last she had something to tell her parents. They were all hypocrites, really. Her father was right. As usual. No wonder he declined all official honour . . .

Meanwhile a giggle threatened. She said, "I've never eaten bacon."

Arranged with geometric precision around the table that was a perfect square, they'd all fallen into sluggishness, but her remarking a difference invoked their uniform background, and an animated discussion on tradition within the bounds of modernity followed.

. . . Entirely as Ceza had predicted.

She longed for Villa Evermor, for its floral stairway carpet. And her feet shod immaculately in nylons and high-heeled shoes felt put upon, as though they'd been lying nude and splintered upon the uneven stoic floorboards.

"Poor Whyte," Ceza said. "He'd probably helped bake the pie, too."

"She couldn't face the thought of a post-mortem."

"And yet I've had the impression that she was so fond of Whyte. She misses him, you know."

"Well, he was the perfect servant."

"But all your mother's servants are excellent —" She added emotionally, "I suppose you were wrong, but you can't really be blamed. I mean, would your mother have been charged, or anything like that?"

"For culpable homicide, at most. At worst she could have got a suspended sentence. If she'd been charged, which I doubt. My father would have done a deal with the prosecutor—after all, it was not premeditated. It was a kind of an accident." He stopped suddenly. "You know, Funnyface, she'd never forgive me for having told you. Nor you for knowing."

"You know you can trust me." She brought her fist to her heart. "No wonder we all went to the funeral."

He said simply, "I'm glad you know."

"You should have told me at the time." She wanted to ask why he had taken her to the funeral. She said instead: "D'you remember the terrible stomach cramps I got while we were driving home?" She remembered their hot, almost silent drive: Sarah resorting to tissues because her supply of Swiss hankies had run out, Paul announcing that he would become a gynaecologist, but she could not recall Whyte's name having been mentioned . . . She now made a great effort not to say anything that might be considered hurtful. Nor would she allow herself to examine all that Paul had told her. It was best not to think about it—but not quite possible . . . She imagined Sarah in the witness box of the court she had been in only that morning . . .

She felt that insistent irrational tiredness again.

It seemed that a scarf, a frey greasy roll of soft flesh-smelling cloth had lodged in her mind. She said, "Do you really think you'll be able to prevent them from publishing those photographs?"

3

Paul did not succeed in preventing all the newspapers from publishing Ceza's photograph. Fortunately, the papers that mattered (the English press) agreed to withdraw all of Ceza's pictures. Not even Ceza saw those. But the Afrikaans papers accommodated Paul by not mentioning her name though she and Thomas of course — that was the whole point — sprawled across their front pages. These Ceza preserved, like pressed flowers, between the pages of *Swift's Anglo-Saxon Primer*. She studied them with what she knew was an unsuitable attention, all but outwearing the paper they were printed on, testing and measuring until she understood that it was her own likeness which so absorbed her. For she considered the photographs as she would a crossword puzzle, always concentrating on the fit. But the fit was of a man and a woman, and Ceza still saw herself as a girl . . . The woman in the photograph then, contemplated the man with an immensity which suggested she might have believed herself to have been assembled by him; the large dark glasses, if only by their absurd failure, exposed . . . The man, for his part, pursued only the camera. His features hugged their defiance tightly, irately, transforming injury into faith. The photographers had somehow trapped a certain stillness in him, and it was in this stillness that Ceza hovered. She looked for him on the campus, but did not like to make any open enquiry. She never found him — her life went on as before.

The beginnings of autumn were noted, but more by the calendar than by physical changes. Leaves dropped, gently, singly; as unrushed as Ceza's days. Sometimes a chill hovered in the sunlight, but never for long, and the sun soothed shoulders that never got tired of the warmth they took for granted.

It was all peacefully dizzying, Ceza found, when she waited on the steps for Paul to fetch her. They'd fallen into the habit of lunching every day — the university was convenient to Paul's rooms, to his little flat. They seemed unable to offend one another. What was there to trouble them — ? Paul's career was decided, happily he would not even have to leave the country to get his additional degree. It was only in deference to her age that Paul had not yet spoken to Philip: her nineteenth birthday was still some months away.

Whyte became, for Paul, a landmark of peace.

Every other Friday night Ceza and Paul dined with the Goodmans. No one — except perhaps Sarah — quite knew how the arrangements had, with such permanence, come about. Still, there it was: a habit that had grown around a ritual and a ritual that had grown around an expectation. Ceza, for example, never came empty-handed, an achievement which engaged a good deal of Irene and Jessica's time and ingenuity. For if gift-giving had become standard, nothing was to be construed as thoughtlessness. Jessica confected her most superior cakes and chocolate truffles and Jacob devoted himself to the rarer blooms of their garden — Birds-of-Paradise, a protea that was especially difficult to grow in the Transvaal, if only because Irene knew that the excellence of her staff would reflect on Ceza. Even so, Irene took careful precautions against appearing mean — a collection of only home-grown gifts would certainly have seemed ungenerous and even worse. Irene therefore propitiated with things like a small, and, of course, rare piece of Sèvres porcelain, or a Lanvin scarf, of bath salts; always biting her lip, though, against the possibility of appearing ostentatious. It was hard to decode the line between the mean and the flashy. But the gifts were a sort of attachment of Ceza's, like, say, her smile.

The right idea came suddenly. She decided on a book. After all, Sarah had been to university.

As it turned out, the book, *Johannesburg Gardens,* was something of a mistake. Sarah's old house and its garden was, unfortunately, included.

"How wonderful to have Pine Lodge given so much space," Sarah said, almost too affably, Ceza thought.

"It is a beautiful house," she said warmly.

"It *was,* you mean —" Sarah said, and sighed.

"I'm sure it was nicer when you lived in it," Ceza said, conscious of looking for the proper thing to say.

Sarah half shrugged, "*Eh, bien,*" she said.

And Ceza could not miss the reproach Sarah aimed at Paul.

"It *must* have been more beautiful when you had it," Ceza said helplessly, at fault, ultimately embarrassed. Rather like the way she felt when she sang off key. As if she ought to have been able to do better.

51

There was a small silence. It was clearly Sarah's turn to speak.

Sarah, meanwhile, crossed the thick wine carpet, almost with distaste. She shut the door against the warm servant sounds, against Whyte's incomprehensible absence.

"You must miss Whyte—" Ceza began. She began again, "Even I miss him—what a pity I never met him."

Sarah clucked.

Ceza felt uninvited, even though her gift had been her entrance fee. Yet she sensed that she had the cheap seats; the stoic watchfulness in Sarah's eyes, eyes that were neither hard not soft, became an usher's eyes, consecrated to keeping Ceza in her proper seat. Sarah's mistrust was immutable, as though it had been founded on a law of nature such as death. Ceza wished that Paul had not entrusted her with Sarah's secret; she was certain that Sarah's reaction to knowing that she knew would be more terrible than anyone could have dared predict.

But the sounds of chatter, of amusement, still penetrated the glass kitchen door.

Again the thick wine carpet was crossed. Sarah was past even trying to conceal her irritation. She was still training her servants. Three replacements had come and gone and the fourth seemed no better. Sarah would not rest until she had achieved the efficient docility that she required.

Ceza busied herself with the intriguing occupation of watching Sarah. For she watched her future mother-in-law as if for some clue to herself.

What she found was that Sarah's face seemed wrong for her — it did not fit. Her reproaching eyes ought to have looked greedy; her lipstick, on lips pleated in the conspiracy of life's inconvenience, ought to have been brighter — instead it was pale, the colour of her bedside lamp-shade. It was a face ransacked by something indeterminate about the features, the nose that was neither long nor short, the carefully tended eyebrows that neither sagged nor arched, the lines about the eyes that remarked nothing other than time. Nor did her always moist teeth quite fit; they seemed as artificial as dentures. Only the deeply decreed reproach, stationary yet unfinishable, was concrete.

Sarah, when she came back was almost satisfied. "*Ma chère,*" she said, "Give them a finger and they'll take a hand." She sighed, "It looks as though this one might work out." As if to no one at all she said, "Louis won't be long now."

Paul began to search for his lighter. "Yes, we're waiting for him," he said, and threw Ceza an almost naughty look.

"He's working in his study, isn't he?" Ceza said.

"He's arranging something," Sarah said.

"You'll see just now —" Paul said.

"Secrets."

"Ah — I smell a mystery," Ceza said, twitching after her own rescue.

"It's not a secret — it's a surprise," Sarah said, and managed to infiltrate a rebuke into her laugh. "For you, Ceza."

"For me?"

"A gorgeous surprise."

"Paul, what is it?"

"It won't be long —" Paul said.

"Yes, go and see what your father is doing — what's taking him so long?"

Ceza was left alone with Sarah, and although this had happened to her only once or twice before, she'd already come to dread the unease that took the shape of guilt which filled these moments. She was afraid of a yawn. She cramped the breath she could not help, and then could do nothing against the way it was forced out — in a yawn which meant everything but boredom.

"Don't tell me you don't have an idea of what the surprise is," Sarah said with some archness.

"You mean from Paul — ?"

"Who else?"

"Paul didn't tell me anything —" Ceza felt that Sarah never quite believed anything she said, and accordingly felt as if she'd been caught using Paul's toothbrush.

"Well," Sarah said, letting her know that she was being allowed to get away with it.

When Paul and his father came in, Ceza was radiant with relief.

"As I see it, this may not be an unequivocal surprise," Louis pronounced heartily.

"I think it is, Dad," said Paul.

"Ceza, my hands are still behind my back," the advocate said, as if this were circumstantial evidence, as if he did not have the habit of walking with his hands neatly folded behind his back.

Ceza brought out a laugh.

"I shan't keep you in suspense any longer." And with a flourish he disclosed a cigar box.

Very quickly the box was in Ceza's lap.

"Open it," Sarah said, with a rapt giggle.

But Ceza's hands seemed muddled: the press-stud catch would not unhasp. She took in her own clumsiness, and compounded it. "Paul?" she said discomposedly, glaringly aware of Sarah's scepticism.

"It's easy," Paul said.

The advocate had lined the box with an unevenly trimmed piece of black velvet against which two diamond rings and a prayer book bound in mother-of-pearl reclined. One of the stones was round, and larger than an aspirin; the other was square, its lines flat and scrupulous but about the same size and weight as the round one. Everything in the box was caught by Sarah's orchid-tinted fluorescence. The box was fairly large and had once held dozens of Havanas whose comforting tender scent still lingered. The Goodmans' expectancy, now acute, could not jolt Ceza into words. Her speechlessness reinforced their silence. At last she said, "I don't know what to say —" Her voice quivered tearfully — embarrassment was fortunately mistaken for what was known as emotion.

"Sarah carried that prayer book on our wedding day," the advocate said with conviction.

"Ceza, you must choose one of the rings," Sarah said quickly, as if she thought Ceza might at any moment be the recipient of both.

"But they're both too big," Ceza said weakly.

"Darling, I couldn't have afforded to get you anything as good as these myself. They're flawless, too — like you."

Excessively amiable, and no less serious, Sarah put in, "I've hardly ever worn them. We always planned on giving one of them to Paul's wife. There's a choice, thank God."

"We would have felt ourselves most remiss indeed had we not done this at least," the advocate said gravely.

From the kitchen a shout of laughter rolled into the room.

"How I need Whyte," Sarah said in a low voice, as if she were praying to herself.

"One must not permit anything to spoil this moment," the advocate said irritably.

"I'm sorry," Sarah said miserably. "Aren't you going to try one on, Ceza?"

"Let *me*," Paul said fervently.

The ring fitted exactly.

"It might have been made for you," Sarah said with a mixture of triumph and coyness. She added, "See — we are alike, you and I."

Paul lifted her hand, delicately manoeuvring it, and so effected maximum glitter.

"It'll look better with nail polish," Sarah said. "A gorgeous frosted one —"

"Let's try the other," the advocate suggested.

The round one was removed and the square applied. It was an exact fit — of course — though the glitter was weaker.

"They're both around three carats or so," Sarah said avidly.

"The emerald-cut weighs a bit more — about 3.2 carats, I think."

Ceza wondered what it was that she had been taught. But it seemed there was nothing she could summon, nothing relevant, from her past. At some bleak point in her mind she was aware that this was far from anything she had ever dreamed of but could not now remember how she had dreamed. Above all she must not appear ungrateful. In any case her parents would have found nothing extraordinary about what was going on, nor was

56

it any less natural than the trousseau collection that had begun when Ceza was about ten years old. In fact this was far more normal an acquisition than the degree she was aiming for. Face to face with her expected destiny she picked up the prayer book. The ring acted as a sort of handcuff; she dropped the little book.

Sarah gasped.

"You had better kiss it," Louis instructed Ceza.

Ceza drew the little book to her lips, remembering how she had felt when her mother had once let a prayer book fall to the floor in synagogue, and the stricken frantic kiss her mother had bestowed.

"I'd like to kiss it, too," Sarah said. "I think I should."

"I'm sorry," Ceza said miserably. "I'm so sorry."

Ceza had the little book again. Again she pressed it to her lips. She could not speak. She nodded, however.

"Which one do you like best?" Sarah asked, rather demanded.

"Paul?" Ceza said emptily, almost hopelessly. She did not really believe he would help her — besides she needed her mother's advice.

"Darling — it's for you to decide — Funnyface."

At this Ceza blushed. Such intimacy. She said desperately, and therefore sounded firm, "No, Paul. You choose."

"You're sure?"

"Yes."

"I like the square one best. What do you think?"

"I think they're both too good for me —" Ceza said. Satisfied that she had, at last, said the right thing she felt her energy revive . . . She was able to place a kiss on Sarah's hard cheek, on the advocate's smooth one, and finally connected with Paul's lips.

Then Whyte's replacement brought the champagne and glasses that had been waiting in the kitchen.

The champagne was not cold enough.

Whyte's death might have brought about this engagement, Sarah believed. Ceza had come in, as it were, at Whyte's funeral. Sarah, who knew she was no fool, knew that much — she could not help also knowing that Paul was to all intents and purposes making a very good match, one that entirely befitted his status as a professional man, a medical man who would be a gynaecologist . . . Whyte's death nevertheless interfered, and Sarah, in her pre-moral way, could not forgive him. Deprived of his gracious services, deprived of his undeniable class, something of the Goodman prestige had emphatically gone — as if they hadn't lost enough when they'd been forced to sell their house! Besides, Sarah had now persuaded herself that Whyte was the only human being she'd not been afraid to trust: his death, and the way he'd died, proved how wrong she had been: in any case, with trust there was mystery, and who but a fool would want that? Well, she was rid of mystery and in its place there was absolutely nothing.

Doing what was expected gave Ceza's life its validity. Nor was she expected to think for herself, any more than Paul was — outside of his career, that is. Their home would be a perfectly balanced compromise between the Steele and the Goodman styles. Not one of the four parents would not feel at home; how could they not — when the new home would be nothing but an extension of the nurseries that had housed Ceza's and Paul's prams? The fulfilment of something even greater than hope. She knew what she must do — she must add to the fervour, so bringing it to fruition. She must wake Irene and Philip, present them with her ring: their night clothes would augment and even seal the event of her engagement. It would be done in their own newly-decorated bedroom, among Philip's office keys and Irene's cosmetics. Yet, that Ceza and Paul were engaged in some kind of complicity that would, before long, scurry them into consanguinity was not yet grasped by either, even though an unspoken, almost unthought yet automatic, agreement took them both to the Steele's bedroom instead of to their little love-making flat after the advocate's serious and formal blessing. And what they were about to perpetuate would receive the distinctive, the infallible, approval of their parents' circles — officially stamped with barely-containable envy. Nothing was missing. There was immunity as well as exposure, well-timed, it would yet surprise.

The diamond of course was exclaimed over, pronounced upon — though its glitter in Irene's room was considerably lessened. (Irene was a follower of discreet lighting.) A gold cigarette case was hastily procured for Paul from Philip's collection, from the Chubb-locked drawer (the only really private one in the house) where his valuables included a revolver. Irene had covered herself in her emerald velvet dressing-gown, but Philip, now endorsing Paul as family, made no effort to cover his underpants.

Ceza and Paul were at the edge of Irene's bed, and her head still practised its new public place on his shoulder. And because no one in her family would wish her luck or even give utterance to that sorcerous word, Ceza, during the next thirty or so minutes of their exactingly expected togetherness, tried and failed in all her effort to be lulled from something oddly connected to fear. She shied away from the recognition of doubt. After all, why should she think for herself? Who was she to have any sort of judgement at all? In any case she was enclosed in the unmistakable brilliance that was faultlessly cast by her ring, and under its aegis their future was not only protected but feverishly assured. It was larger than Irene's own engagement ring and almost as large as Irene's largest rings, as was proper — Ceza's life would naturally be better, greater and presumably longer than that of her parents. Irene and Philip had done everything to make her believe that this was why they were alive. Just as Ceza was an inevitable beneficiary of what is called progress so her children would have still more, still better.

After a while, Irene remembered. The inter-com was out of order. But there was an alternative. She pushed the ormolu button that was encrusted in turquoise and grey ersatz pearls, three pushes and, though it would be heard in all the servants' rooms, Jessica would know it was for her. It was almost midnight. "We must have champagne!" she said, rather, called, looking at Philip, who hated to have the servants disturbed after hours, willing him to recognize and pass, for once, the breaking of one of his edicts.

"Of course we must," Philip agreed warmly. "I'll fetch it myself."

"I've already rung the bell —" Irene said in the gay way she used whenever she wanted to warn Philip not to spoil things.

"Pity," Philip said. He could not avoid clicking his tongue.

"But Jessica would want to be here," Ceza filled in

quickly. "She'd feel left out — she'll have some champagne with us."

And Jessica, when she entered, looked askew, unfamiliar, dimensionless. Her grey uniform fused, as it was meant to, with Irene's newly-redecorated room that the director (the same man who had "done out" Philip's offices) had styled after Picasso's *Symphonie en gris,* yet seemed disturbed. Her wonderfully large breasts unusually uncased were felt, in a sense, by all of them. Jessica clapped her hands, said Au, Au, repeatedly, applauding the ring.

"The first time I met you, Jessica, you didn't have your apron on either," Paul said. He winked at Ceza. "Remember, Funnyface?"

She felt tired again, and longed to rest her head, to fall asleep once more, one last time, against Jessica's breasts. Because she felt she was being forced into womanhood, and so deflected this injustice against Sarah's ring which ought not to have fitted in such an uncompromising way. She'd have it reset, anyway. As if to guard herself against these meddlesomely irrelevant thoughts, she smiled her powerfully innocent smile.

"Well, Jessica, you'll have to start looking for a girl for Miss Ceza. An experienced cook —" Irene declared as if to imply that this was one of the difficulties (necessary evils?) that was the real stuff of marriage. She added, "I can't believe all this —"

"We thought you'd be cross if we didn't tell you," Ceza said graciously. "So we woke you up."

"I'll go and make you some tea," Jessica said knowledgeably.

"Champagne would be better —" Irene offered.

"I'll bring it up."

61

Authoritatively rather than dismissively, Irene said, "As quick as you can —"

"You're going to have some too —" Ceza said.

Jessica demurred.

"But you must," Ceza said agitatedly.

"Of course she will —" Philip said firmly.

The silver bucket and crystal glasses appeared with almost undue speed and, cased (or caged?) in her apron, Jessica was once more the known, the safe, the unchangeable nanny of Ceza's childhood.

And when they drank their champagne, Jessica's chipped and battered enamelled servant's cup did not obtrude, rather it consolidated the moment.

Irene went happily ahead with her trousseau buying, Jessica discussed, planned and revised the menu for the long-anticipated guests — Advocate and Mrs. Louis Goodman. Philip's business had proliferated — he now had an architectural and planning department to deal with their ever-spreading branches, a statistical department to deal with stock control, as well as the most advanced computer in South Africa. He scarcely recognized the place that made him feel powerful yet placeless. His office had been professionally redecorated, and he felt uncomfortable in it, and used a small cubicle whenever he could.

4

A lecturer returned from a sabbatical. His name was unadorned: no Ph.D., no professor. He required no self-distinguishing title, which rather upset Ceza's notion of the way things went. His name was Mr. Cowley and he kept about him a kind of macintosh haze; expected nothing, but was prepared. He was lazy, too, and conducted his classes by questioning; prepared for everything yet would not himself prepare lectures. He sat on the podium and turned the pages of his file slowly, as if in the interstices there were an assembly of wisdom, if not truth. He'd discovered the difference. And when he flung his discovery at Ceza she clutched hold of it in wonderment. The pages contained little — a list of the shape of her mother's grocery orders was all that Ceza could make out. Mr. Cowley held there was no teaching, only learning. This was his entire educational philosophy. Since he could not teach, they would learn. He preferred, he announced, to mark and even to read essays: almost anything was preferable to the delivery of ponderous lectures that would only be dropped like unhatchable eggs. He would express the acuities of his intellect in bitter little marginalia: "contents duly noted, though not well understood," or "my fascination has been

63

aroused: you went so cleverly off the point, the makings, indeed, of a true diplomat." He never awarded an "A." His voice was monotonous, yet delicate, like his lips, like the evenness of his complexion, but, like the contents of the unsaid, it absorbed. Watching him, Ceza began to delve depths in herself that she had not suspected. For all her long political discussions with her father, neither had ever read the *New Statesman,* nor had they heard of the *Observer,* nor even, and perhaps more surprisingly, of the *Economist.*

Experience sat on the edge of the crest-ring that illuminated Mr. Cowley's little finger — like language, it could be translated, though not, he hoped, to the illiterate. Or so Ceza assumed. He held his lectures in the carpeted senate room, which gave them the solemnity that Ceza mistook for profundity. She began, for the first time, to work in an honest way and neglected other subjects.

Perhaps it amused Mr. Cowley to use ridicule to inspire; Ceza certainly benefited. He had uncovered, in front of the whole class, the fact that she had not known that Gandhi had once lived and worked in her home town.

"Perhaps," he said, "Mr. Shalali will take Miss Steele in hand? Perhaps over a cup of coffee he could tell her, if she would consent to grace the student canteen, something about African nationalism?"

When she blushed, he'd been gratified; she knew. Ah, yes — he'd summed her up — she knew that when she detected the faint flush of contempt she saw whenever he noticed her. She was sure he saw her innocence as manufactured.

It was as if he'd got to the truth of her and knew it all.

Why, at the merest glance, her impeccably pink finger-nails gave her away as an ordinary collection of varnish, cream and dressmakers.

On one of her essays, departing from his custom, Mr. Cowley noticed something personal: "This is the work of a little badge of benevolence. See me!" She waited for him nervously. She chided herself for her nervousness — even Advocate Goodman had informed her that Mr. Cowley was a failed advocate who had not been able to make a living in civvy street; he'd never had two pennies to rub together. But when she was seated opposite him in his austere and somehow tinlike office (barren of every-thing but books), her mind discarded Advocate Good-man's assessments. She received what Mr. Cowley said with the kind of shameless delight that is felt bodily, for it was her mind he was discussing. He told her that she might just become one of his better students. He said she could be more than a little badge of benevolence, more than a ready-made plutocrat (at this Ceza was reminded of the scarf she had borrowed that day in court), but warned her that she'd have to realize, somehow, that the rest of the world was not behind the thick barricade of family blood that threatened her with extinction. She was, he cautioned, allowing her mind to be nothing but a cage for waste. But of course she could remain an affluent bone, needlessly passing the time, that was her preroga-tive. She could, on the other hand, take advantage of her undoubted abilities. She had definite potential.

And so Ceza overcame Irene's, and later Paul's objec-tions, and no longer wore nail varnish. She also made a little more use of the libraries.

Ceza supposed, afterwards, that but for Mr. Cowley, and

the dressmaker, Mrs. Visser, she would not have known that she had no real with to marry. It seemed somehow providential that two such unlikely people, distant from one another, and remote from her world — should have been the one who — as Irene would have said — influenced her.

Mr. Cowley had inspired Ceza. Until then she had considered herself as some kind of luxury in the privileged scheme of things, even though loyalty to the family out-distanced — if not obliterated — loyalty to herself. She'd seen all her academic results as a fluke, an accident; she hadn't expected to do well at university. Because the life of the mind had seemed out of reach and therefore worthless to her. Nor had she been taught to expect anything of herself — all would be done for her. One day she would have to give birth to a child, but even that would be accomplished with maximum help. Mr. Cowley had told her that she had potential; she had not known that such a quality could be relevant (in Mr. Cowley's sense) to her; she had expected to continue, she had not hoped to grow.

The dressmaker, Mrs. Visser, lived close to the university, in a suburb that was not only a suburb — it mixed small houses with large buildings and one or two lesser factories. It had been exclusive, once, but Johannesburg had no use for tradition, and it was something of a semi-slum. Mrs. Visser's verandah steps were as scarlet as her nails; both had lumps from too much polish that looked like overcooked porridge. Mrs. Visser had made Irene's wedding dress, and was, in a sense, the grandmother Ceza had never known, because she was the only elderly lady in their lives. Living had gathered about her — her powdered face was a collision with the chalk she used to mark her materials. Engulfed in bright lipstick, her mouth was a magnet for pins, which was why it was so easy for her to talk with them. Men had sent her lips askew. No male could be trusted — *they* had only to button the fly — even her own son, even her own grandson, too quick to unbutton, spewed grandchildren, and now great-grandchildren all over the place. The Steeles used Mrs. Visser because she was reasonable, and because they were not to be spoilt. "*Who* did Mrs. Visser not know?" Irene used to marvel — meaning that she knew everything about everyone. But Ceza thought: *what* does Mrs. Visser not know — ? She knew everything: her son was in gaol — cheques always, always bouncing, always in trouble. Bad luck. The phrase forbidden in the Steele household, but so deliciously heard in the little tin-roofed house that smelt of cooking gas, of floor polish and of something else that the Steeles could not be expected to identify. Nor had they tried . . . Bad luck it was, while Mrs. Visser her mouth a pin cushion while tears leapt down, bad luck, when her son had stood on the melting tar in the Durban road, holding his dead wife in his arms stone-cold sober after the accident. Passers-by who had stopped to help pinched their suitcases. Yes, Mrs. Visser knew all about life.

Mrs. Visser was more precious than Ceza dared realize; recognition would have been a vice — she did not speak of her — unless you counted discussion of her in her capacity as a dressmaker. Mrs. Visser was an outsider — to have talked of her life would have shrivelled their world. She was like the radio serial they listened to on Saturday mornings, inside the languor of Irene's bedroom, sitting on the window-seat with their backs to the view Irene had created while the sun stroked them through the ivy, glancing off the tall poplars that Irene thought she had just about — well, made; they'd been trans- planted fully grown, but had survived — Mrs. Visser was the real-life drama Ceza could never hope to reach. The powder that veiled the skin, her powdery breath, the knitted ribbing (two plain, two pearl) of the skin be- tween her sagging pin cushion breasts, and always, al- ways through this the gleam of blue, a suspicion, a liquescence of coloured blood. Yet not a servant. Mrs. Visser meant grief, men, love, occasional drunkenness. The real thing — nothing like radio serials.

Ceza went to a fitting without Irene. Which event showed Ceza that the pattern of the future she was so carelessly slipping into had already been cut. She had been letting things happen as if there were no way out of performing what was required of her, as if there were no alternative to the propagation of her parents' hopes.

"That ring of yours is as big as an aspirin," Mrs. Visser said.

Ceza giggled. "I know," she said. She waited for the usual envious sounds.

"I hope you won't always be taking them."

"Taking what?"

"Aspirin. Oh, the ladies I get in here! The bigger the diamond the bigger the headache. Always miserable, always complaining, always sick. Sick headaches."

"Well, I don't think —"

"Who cares what a girl like you thinks," Mrs. Visser interrupted. "What do you know? You've no right to be getting married anyway. It's not that you're eighteen or nineteen — that's okay for a young woman who's earned a few pence, who's been around. But *you*! You know nothing of life. Well — do you?"

"Not really."

"Not really," Mrs. Visser mimicked. "You're a nice girl or I wouldn't bother. What a mother-in-law you're getting! Always asking questions about you." She moved the pins to the other side of her mouth and then took them out. "What about a cup of tea?"

"Love one."

"Come along then."

Ceza was used to kitchens that looked as if they had been designed as small factories or laboratories, suitable for nothing but work. No one Ceza knew actually ate or sat in a kitchen. But this was a real room — clumsy, comfortable and used.

"Been in bed with him?" Mrs. Visser asked companionably.

"Yes."

"Is he a magician?"

"What?"

"I mean is all you can ever think about is making love to him?"

"Oh — no."

"I should have guessed but I thought you were still a virgin."

This was the first time anyone had treated Ceza as an ordinary woman instead of a delicate girl. Accordingly, she felt relaxed and confident and found herself in a pleasurably confiding, and new, mood; she had been longing to be recognized.

"I never thought I'd feel pity for you," Mrs. Visser said.

"And do you?"

"Yes. I'm sorry, but I do. What fun have you had? Okay — so you'll never have to worry about money. But what fun have you had? I have the feeling that you're not really getting married for yourself, but to please your parents. Tell me, am I right?"

Ceza shrugged.

"Thought as much. Of course it's a good match. A big opportunity. A doctor on top of everything. He'll turn you into a very good servant of his. I mean you won't be allowed to have a mind of your own, will you?"

"No."

And Ceza remembered the day she had wanted to cancel the lunch, remembered Paul's disapproval over her having marched in the protest — she'd felt so alive that morning. She drank her tea and saw Paul as heartless — the thought of being struck off the medical register had upset him far more than Whyte's death, or the way he'd died.

Mrs. Visser said, "You've got plenty of time."

"I know."

"They must be good in bed. They're all bastards anyway. Them and their flys. They even have zips now to make things easier for themselves. But what's inside the fly must be good, must work — they must know how to use it!" Mrs. Visser gave a pleasant reminiscent laugh. "The biggest diamonds don't seem to have helped my customers, haven't stopped them from whining. To think they haven't got the sense to know that what they want is a nice big bed, with a nice big man. I pity them."

"You've taught me a lot."

"Well, you're a quick learner. Let's have a look at the ring."

Ceza took it off.

Mrs. Visser held it up to the light. "I wonder how much it costs?" she said.

"I don't know. I'm returning it."

Paul was working that night and she did not have to see him. She realized she'd been seeing him more out of duty than desire.

In the morning she would ask Jessica to let her parents know that she had made up her mind, she would not be getting married. It would be easire than telling them herself.

That grey greasy scarf rolled into her mind. She fell asleep effortlessly.

Jessica sounded the alarm at once.

"But you're not dressed," Ceza said when Philip came into her room.

Jessica and Jonas brought breakfast-trays.

"Don't worry about me. A day at home will do me no harm at all." His voice glanced away. He said, "Cancelled my big meeting. Whatever you decide — we're behind you —" he went on masterfully. "I think I'll open the curtains, don't you? We need some light on the subject."

Ceza shaded her eyes, but the curtains were flung wide and, though it was winter, summer rushed in. Ceza shaded her eyes with both hands.

"Try to eat, darling —" Irene said lightly, only half-pleadingly.

"Yes," Philip said approvingly. "You should try to eat. No sense getting ill. You'll need all your strength." He turned to Irene. "Of course she'll eat," he said.

Ceza complied.

The others ate too.

"Careful of the bones," Philip said automatically. "Now Ceza, what you feel is only normal. We want your happiness. All girls go through this sort of thing. Your mother cancelled our marriage two days before it was to take place. Did you know that?"

Ceza nodded.

"Look at us now. We don't even remember what the quarrel was all about. No idea. Is that right, Irene?"

Irene murmured.

"You see?" Philip said. "Good. We know where we stand. We like Paul, as you know. But that shouldn't count. We think you're a good pair. But that shouldn't count either. We know you'd never marry anyone we didn't approve of —"

With practised concurrence Ceza said, "Absolutely."

"So we agree," Philip wound on. "But I'm in no hurry to get rid of you, my girl. Now, Ceza, we don't want to interfere — we know it's your own life — but what was the quarrel about?"

"There has been no quarrel."

"He loves you so much," Irene said, making it obvious that she could not help saying it. She sighed her disbelief.

"You must have quarrelled," Philip insisted. He added he thought wisely, "Between you and me, I think Paul must have tried to do something impulsive. Only natural. I'm a man — I understand these things —"

"Paul doesn't know it's off —" Ceza said weakly.

"You must be crazy, Ceza." Irene laughed daintily. "So it's not so serious, after all."

"But I'm not marrying him. I've hardly slept a wink," Ceza said to affirm her astonishing announcement. Then, as if a new thought had just struck her, she said softly, "I'm too young—"

"Same age as I was—" Irene exclaimed.

Ceza gave a long shudder. She said, "I can't remember what he looks like—"

His photograph was handed to her.

They waited avidly while she studied it. It was his nose she fastened on—that passive geometric sculpture—that symbol of feminine vanity. A critical sound issued—from her teeth, it seemed. She said, "Is he really *so* good-looking. I can't remember—"

Philip said to his wife, "All this is too much strain for her—" He winked. "I don't like it. I don't like it one bit."

But Irene waved him away. "He's very good-looking, darling."

Ceza made an indistinct movement of her shoulders. She said petulantly, "I can't remember."

"We should get a doctor for her," Philip said.

"But Paul's a doctor, for God's sake. What more could you want."

"I don't like it one bit. Not one little bit. She seems —I don't know—sort of—well, it looks as if she's sort of—well—disturbed—" said Philip, floundering.

Irene made a lulling sound. "She's all right," she said with authority. "She'll return to her senses—"

Philip swallowed in a final way. "She ate at least," he said. "Well, Ceza, you had something to eat at least."

Ceza neatened her eiderdown and drew it further toward her chin. This, by way of answer. An unstinted yawn spread along her face. She contemplated her vacant left hand. "It's *so* bright," she said.

73

"Can we close the curtains, Dad?" asked Ceza.

"Just this once," Philip said. He added — "You know how I hate the dark — In the meantime we should ring for Jessica. Okay, Ceza?"

The bell was obediently pressed.

"Why have trays in the bedroom —" Philip continued. He liked, in all crises, to prove that life went on.

Jessica, who had been waiting outside Ceza's room, appeared immediately. Her buttocks seemed to waddle in time with her sympathetic clucks. "Au — Miss Ceza —" she said. "Poor Miss Ceza —"

"We must leave her to rest." He stood up. "Ceza, you'll tell Paul about this yourself, I take it. I think we all agree that you shouldn't say anything to Paul just yet. You should sleep on it. I'll leave your mother with you. Women's talk."

Sounding openly embarrassed, though no less ashamed, Ceza said, "I can't bear it when he touches me. He's not always kind —"

Because Irene was unreservedly ready to soothe.

"I knew there was a really important reason."

"He revolts me."

While Ceza spoke, Irene, as she did so often, mouthed her words.

"But in what way, darling?"

Ceza said conclusively, "Physically."

Irene said tightly, "Sarah Goodman will never forgive you. She has an unforgiving heart." Tentatively, she added, "In the end, you know, a woman gets used to a man. You won't always find him revolting . . . He's a good man —"

"I'm *so* tired," Ceza said.

Paul came.

They sat on cane chairs on the long lazy verandah. It was mildly autumnal, and the grass had mellowed to a comforting yellow. Ceza's ring was where it belonged but was being twisted.

"Is it too tight?" Paul said.

"In a way—"

"What way?" he said sharply.

"I don't fit it—"

"Look — I'm not following you too well—"

"I suppose not."

"What's got into you?"

She crushed her fists against her eyes and saw a kaleidoscope of fire-light yellows. She said, "Please."

Paul pulled her fists away. "Funnyface," he said tenderly, "what's the matter?"

She would not open her eyes. She said drearily, "Please—" But allowed her hand to rest passively in both of his. "Please — try to understand—"

"I'm trying—"

How could he not have any idea? She blamed him for it, thought him "thick." And was then even more oppressed by her own callousness. Still, he ought to have known more, and, because he clearly did not, she believed *she'd* been tricked — worse, swindled. Was he or was he not *nine years* older than she? She opened her eyes. Defenceless, she assessed quickly, immature. And snapped them shut. He was stiff with disbelief, suddenly his hands fluttered with their old childishness; a crisis of hurt collected and quivered slowly in him, like the beginnings of loneliness.

She said, "I'm too young. I can't possibly go through with this." And heard the almost sordid cut of her voice.

Appalled, she took his hands, and quietened them. "Don't you see — I'm too young —"

"But you're eighteen."

"You see," she said in a low yet victorious tone, "You don't understand."

"Does your mother know about this?" he asked.

"Yes. They all know."

"They all know —"

"They think I'm mad —"

If only he'd get angry, she wished. Or seem passionate. He was not only defenceless but defeated. Why couldn't he at least make it easier for her — and what had he done with his pride, his honour, anyway? She answered him because she had to, because she could never face being rude, but very soon the pitch of her real awareness was flung against her fatigue — that exquisite fatigue harnessed to a dimensionless dislike of hurting him, of hurting anyone. She half-suspected it was this and not the other that had so spuriously passed for love that had rushed her into all this. Her body had messed her up she decided, though even now, inexcusably, she could barely remember his love-making. Why not? Why did it seem like those forgotten moments before an accident? And yet in a way her liaison with him had been horribly accidental, searchlights of approval notwithstanding.

It occurred to her that she might lose her virginity again. Ah, she thought, the next and final time would become the real time. No more accidents. Now his tears saddened and at the same time disgusted her. But for a dying grandfather — who, for God's sake, was entitled — she'd never seen a man weep before. Her disgust pointed to her tenderness. She smoothed his tears with her own handkerchief.

She knew she wasn't worth crying over, and he ought to have had the sense, at least, to see that . . . Oh, he was weak . . . Pity spread but only in direct proportion to loathing, for each . . . The temptation to marry him fibrillated, but would not be palliated. She said, hopelessly, she thought: "I'm too young."

Just then, Irene, who could no longer withstand not knowing what was going on, clattered onto the verandah carrying a tray of iced pineapple juice that she had made herself. "I hope I'm not interrupting anything —" she remarked, more or less warily, but wanting Paul to know she knew.

Past the formality of standing, Paul said awkwardly, "Your daughter is sending me away."

"My daughter doesn't know what she is doing —" Irene replied firmly, as if there were no more to be said, as if Paul ought to know this, and accordingly should dismiss it all as so much nonsense. Ceza, she was certain, would then be brought to her senses.

At this, Ceza felt a sudden sense of homelessness — she could not recall ever feeling anything like anger — worse, like outrage — against her mother before. The newness of this ultimately forbidden sensation was also her closest link with real sin. Beaming her fullest horror upon her mother she said, "*Mommy!*" It was a simple enough reaction, yet was uttered with too much force to be retrieved. And in that everything became final.

"It's true, Ceza —" Irene said. "You don't know what you're doing."

"Hadn't you better leave us?" Ceza asked.

And her voice, so oddly virtuous with purpose, was obeyed.

When they were on their own Paul said, "She didn't

deserve that." He added bitterly, "You shouldn't hurt your own mother as well." He meant to pierce. "She's the sort whom no one has the right to hurt!"

"I suppose *you* think I'm enjoying myself!" Ceza said huntedly. "That would be typical of you!"

She'd got him on the raw — in spite of herself.

He said unequivocally, "Professional men are at a premium, you know —"

"Is that so —?" A short disordered laugh scurried off her lips. "In that case I never *was* good enough — You'd have got less than you're worth!" Unable to contain an overwhelming relief, she leaned toward him. "Now I know what I'm doing. Thanks to you."

He went on as if he hadn't heard. "And you're sending me away. Your mother's right — you can't know what you're doing." He took her hand but again applied no pressure — it lay in his unfeelingly — a glove would have lent more sensation. He said quietly, "Look — Funny-face — I've made love to you, but no one will ever know —"

"And I won't tell anyone about the chicken-mushroom pie," she added scornfully. "Don't worry, your secret's safe with me."

She'd taken great gulps of weariness, a lump of congealed sleep struck the backs of her eyes. Relentlessly she roused herself. She said, "The announcement — you know — for the paper —? Can we say the engagement has been cancelled by mutual consent?"

Sounding unconquerably hopeless, he said, "You're way ahead of me, Funnyface. Do what you like —"

Patrolled by her family's quiet deferences to what they were sure she must be feeling, Ceza's exhaustion very quickly awakened into an aliveness that was not quite a vitality nor yet joyous; it was simply the pleasure of rolling back into their wings. Rolling so thoroughly as to become eclipsed. All unpleasant details were sucked away; nor was any nerve exposed. Sleep more than met her half-way, of course, for she complied with their urgent pleas to rest. And of Philip's dealings with the Goodmans nothing was said. Ceza's enquiries were weak enough, but they were treated as if they had been passionate pleas; she was exhorted to be calm, not to distress herself for nothing and no one was worth such pain.

Ceza accepted the convalescence she knew she didn't need uncomplainingly. Because it was uncertain whether the smart behind Irene's eyes was due to Ceza's failuer to bring off all that glory, or to the pain and even shame she believed her to be suffering.

Before long other young men began to invite her out. But she did not accept, partly because they seemed mere boys and partly because she thought it unseemly; her new-found (unpolished) heartlessness was not something she cared to display. Something other than a counterfeit of illusion ought to animate her body, now kept under constant deluge by way of incessant needless showers. Thus scalded and chilled, her complexion assumed a defenceless touching whiteness, and with it her innocence spiralled. And in that immemorial conspiracy that proclaims youth and innocence one (as if ageing is the one and only plunderer), even Irene came to draw comfort from the belief that Ceza was indeed too young — for what quality is quite so persuasive as innocence?

Monday morning, and Sarah sat at her nostalgic desk as usual. She contemplated a bright cook-book whose dust jacket was blistered with careless handling and against which her nose wrinkled in acute distaste. She thought of ringing for Judith, her newest cook, but decided not to — she couldn't bear to face that slut whose over-sized breasts wore through overalls in no time at all. There was nothing of the piquant in cooking, now that Whyte was gone, taking the flavour of her kitchen with him . . . Her sister Doris had gone too, to Europe, almost with relief, Sarah thought, even though she knew how much she was needed . . . And Ceza who had come in at Whyte's death — a bad omen to begin with! — had gone, too.

It all seemed pointless. She'd been born without any notion of having faith in faith; when Whyte died she took Bible classes which she dropped in disgust. No matter how much she whined and nagged and raged against herself, all the self-disapproval in the world could not convince her that it was absurd to carry on about a stranger, leave alone a servant! Ah, if only Whyte could see her now! There was nothing to reinforce her face, and, though she still diligently applied primary colours they were nothing but artificial dabs on a shroud.

Her pink bedroom curtains were drawn against the light. But she was at her desk. She wished she'd been the type who could stay in bed till noon — but no, there she was, dressed, she supposed, immaculately, sitting at a three-hundred-year-old desk thinking of — what? — she couldn't be sure — The menus were no more than a pretence.

Odd, though. When she wasn't thinking of Whyte, she was thinking of Ceza. She knew more about that little bitch than she would ever let on. She wondered what Ceza knew of her; sometimes she thought that Paul might have told her about the pie.

If only she could forget about the night when Philip Steele had presented himself, without even having bothered to telephone in advance. What if they'd been out? Or had had guests?

When the door bell rang she had answered it, of course. Louis never answered bells of any sort in his own home. Even when he sat by the telephone he refused to answer. Said phones were uncivilized. Well, there stood Philip Steele looking for all the world as if he'd come to break some bad news — his shirt seemed to be too wide in the collar. Sarah couldn't help sounding urgent. "What's wrong?" she said.

"I wish I knew —" he answered vaguely. He went on more determinedly, as if it had just occurred to him that Sarah, and even Louis, did not know that anything was amiss. Unless, of course, they thought nothing had gone wrong, that they were pleased with Paul's broken engagement. Impossible. Still, he'd never understood the woman who now stood reproachfully before him.

"I'd like to have a word with both you and Louis," Philip said, already making his way to Louis's sacred study. It was a professional room, but that, as Sarah noted, was hardly designed to deter the likes of Philip Steele.

She followed him, but when she should have been anxious, she was only curious. Ah, how she let herself down sometimes.

"Ah, Philip. Good to see you, if I may say so —"

"Then you at least know why I'm here?"

"No." Louis made a deprecatory gesture. "But it's always good to see you. After all . . ."

Here Philip interrupted. Sarah thought she would never be able to forget his expression. His look of desperate misery, with his mouth moving as though its teeth itched, was scarcely different from the stockbroker who had swindled them, but who had behaved as though he was the swindled one. Philip said, "Between you and me, there's no 'after all' anymore. That's finished."

"You'd better sit down," Louis said briskly. "You too, Sarah." His voice suddenly quickened, jarred — "There hasn't been an accident — ?"

"*Dieu me garde,*" Sarah murmured.

"No, thank God," Philip said staunchly.

"Perhaps we should talk over a drink?" Louis said while he moved deftly to the butler's tray that always gleamed with an implacable readiness to serve. Sarah had found sparkling ancient Spanish decanters for it; she looked upon them covetously even now, even though they belonged to her. She'd probably give one to Ceza. "Of course, you don't drink, Philip. I'd almost forgotten."

"I will tonight," Philip answered. He seemed determined to handle the situation amicably, so determined that he didn't care whether it showed. Sarah noted that, and knew, fatalistically that she would be unable not to hold it against him.

"Let's give you some of this malt whiskey. It's twenty-five years old."

Philip could not conceal his impatience. "Wasted on me, of course," he said with the contempt he always felt for people who were concerned with wines and the like. He recovered himself. He said, "Though it's very nice of you —" He was thinking: "I head a vast business. An empire. A monster. I made it all. And how? By getting down to brass tacks and not by this effete business of long business lunches, and polite talk over malt whiskey.

Still, if I can handle literally millions I can handle this for my daughter." He said, "I must say this is an excellent whiskey."

"In that case we must present you with a bottle," Louis said firmly. "Sarah?" But she was already up and brandishing those keys that were so essential to all housewives, as Philip knew.

"That's not—" Philip began. Then, "How kind of you—" Why not let Louis score this one point?

"It's our pleasure. If not for our new family, then for whom?" Louis scowled in the well-cultivated way that signalled he was about to get down to business.

Which was not lost on Philip.

"I didn't think it would fall to me to have to tell you. Hasn't Paul said anything? No—Well then perhaps he doesn't believe it either—" He halted, appeared to be searching his memory, took a pettish sip and then another. The long minute went by without interruption. "Ceza has . . . that is, they've cancelled their engagement. They are no longer engaged—"

A profoundly reluctant sound, like a gently punctured vein seemed to perforate Sarah's breath.

"I'm sorry—" Philip said sadly.

All notion of urbane attention slid away from Louis. He said, "But we know nothing of this." He turned to his wife as if he thought this was another of he secrets. "Did Paul say anything to you, Sarah?"

"Not a word. I'd no idea."

"And when, if the former bridegroom's father might be allowed to ask—did all this come about?"

"Two days ago. On Tuesday."

"I see. Well of course that explains it . . . A lovers'

83

quarrel, of course. For all you know they're probably together at this very moment," Louis said patiently, fetching up a dusty laugh.

Philip had been lighting his cigar but stopped before the flame had caught. "I'm afraid not," he said and resumed his puffing.

"Do you know why?" Louis asked somewhat sourly.

Philip shook his cigar in time with his head. "We're not pleased, you know —"

"Sarah — what do you make of all this? The territory of the heart is more a woman's geography than a man's."

In answer she flung him an irritated glance that was meant to cut off his line of questioning.

Louis would not be put off. He said, "Well then — does this not come as a surprise to you, too? Clearly Ceza's father has been taken aback —"

"Not altogether —" meditated Sarah. "No, I can't say I'm altogether surprised. No, not at all —"

"Why not?" Philip asked at once, with more than a hint of having been slighted.

"That's not something I can explain — even to myself —" She winced. "Perhaps you should tell us what you know."

"Of course I will," Philip waved his cigar. "I hardly know myself. She's returned the ring. I mean he's got the ring. Irene told him that she thought Ceza didn't know what she was doing —" Almost wistfully, he broke off.

"I see. Am I to assume that Ceza broke it off?" Louis asked. "This sort of thing is bound to happen. She's only a youngster, you know, and there is every reason to believe —"

Now Philip broke in. "That's what Ceza says. She's informed us all that she's too young — Can't understand

84

it myself. Her mother was expecting her when she was the same age." He turned to Sarah for support. "You too, I suppose?"

"No, I was two years older —"

"She was completing her studies," Louis said, making it clear that none of this was of any relevance at all. He said suddenly, "I wonder how Paul feels?"

A vicious shudder toppled Sarah's shoes into one another. She said, "We were out to dinner last night. Didn't we have the law society banquet? Honestly, I can't remember — he left a message with Judith that he wouldn't be in —"

Philip intervened protectively. This sort of thing can't be easy for a mother, he thought. He said, "Ceza's been resting in bed. She's done nothing but sleep and eat —" He was suddenly aware of Sarah. An even greater unease.

Sarah said unexpectedly, "I was most fond of your daughter."

He heard something accusing in her tone and said at once, "There's no one else —" Odd, the possibility hadn't occurred to him before.

Sarah appeared to withdraw her attention. She heard, without interest, the discussion over the announcement of their cancelled engagement. Louis would see to the wording, and his messenger would convey it to Philip who would do whatever was necessary.

Inasmuch as Sarah could think of anything, she thought of Whyte. She ached to discuss Ceza with him . . .

Later that night they'd confronted Paul, of course. But here Sarah's impressions had blurred. She'd watched Paul speak, but her mind had jammed.

The worst thing of all was that Paul told them he

didn't want to live with them any longer. He'd be moving, he said, the next day. A friend of his had given him a small flat . . . For the time being.

Sarah had expected Ceza to telephone, at least. She'd waited for days, planning and replanning what she would say to her. But there was no contact from anyone in the Steele family. Not even Irene, and this final disappointment had emptied Sarah of everything. Even scorn . . .

5

And then, one morning, Johannesburg experienced snow.

For Ceza that morning was moist with perpetuity, and so prominent in her consciousness that it permitted infinite surprise. The snow had seduced professors into cancelling lectures, and alone with Indra, Ceza had watched the snow drop in forgiving flakes against his skylight, until the grimed glass became a white wall. Then, discloistered, and lying with him on his pseudo-slum bed, when even the sustained weeping from the room next door was no more than another lulling sound, she knew that it was not just that she had begun another affair which so overwhelmed her, nor even that Indra was not white — the strange thing was that he was not a Jew. *That* seemed to be the point, the whole point; and in the kind of panic which burst safes, she had turned to him, and in her wild drive to expel her water-tight blooded legacy, she'd shocked them both.

They'd transcended the bounds of ordinary secrecy, of ordinary conspiracy; they'd become lawless. Ceza was not sure when it was that she began watching for Indra's immaculate university blazer. She half believed that it was some time before she'd let herself in for that protest march. She longed to ask when he'd noticed her, but knew instinctively that she must not. In any case, he was asleep, though restlessly, almost uncomfortably. His head moved, rather sprang, about the pillow, as if it would never be palliated, still less, settled. She ached to soothe him, and to calm, and knew — resoundingly — that there was nothing she would not do and that because he'd left her senseless (as he would always?) she would never have enough to give him. His nostrils twitched. As if to apply a compress she would have touched his forehead yet forced herself not to; an uninvited touch now seemed unchaste, overfamiliar. His clothes spilled over the chair and on to his desk — she observed them minutely and was certain that she was as aware of their arrangement as of a jigsaw puzzle many times completed. But her own clothes, sent skidding across the room by him, would not easily tolerate her gaze. The skirt and cashmere pullover embarrassed her; she wondered whether she would ever be able to place her clothes alongside his, but the question slipped from her mind and gave way to the real problem of how and when they would be able to meet again. Would it be as easy the next time? Would there be a next time?

It had begun so simply.

She'd been standing on those university steps watching the students fooling with the miraculous snow when he'd asked her to come to his place.

"Where?" she heard herself say matter-of-factly.

"Cross Street."

He took her books. "I have a car," he said.

"I know. I've seen it."

"Uh huh—"

But they were walking towards the parking lot. She wondered how her legs could move. Then they drove silently. He said once, "To think the populace are concerned over whether or not to have a state lottery. Ludicrous, isn't it?"

She said mechanically, "Of course." A little later, she repeated too fervently, as if she were learning a new word, "Ludicrous. Quite ludicrous."

Ceza knew Cross Street well. Once, it had been a Sunday outing for the family — the buying of fresh fruit and vegetables on Sunday mornings had been something of a ritual that had only been abandoned when the Indian "Sammy" brought his green vegetable truck to Villa Evermor. The street, even then, had excited her, if only because the always-crying children always cried differently. The unexpected memory of those sounds (wailing, not crying, she now realized) was dizzying, and she almost tumbled from the car when he opened the door for her. All her concentration was invested in walking; much in the way she had once pushed out her tongue, she tiptoed.

"There's no need to walk like that," he said irritably. "There's a very fashionable Hindu dressmaker here. You can always say that's where you went if anyone sees you!"

"Yes." She wanted to tell him that she hadn't even thought of being seen until he mentioned it, that she felt dizzy with disbelief. The earlier memory that had crowded her ears was forgotten. She thought she saw someone who looked like Sarah, but put that down to suggestion. She tendered a laugh, "You've made me nervous," she said.

He walked more briskly.

His keys jangled.

Locking the door he said mildly, "Well, this is it. It may not be grand. But it's mine. And private."

He would tell Ceza later — much later — that his father owned the building. The room had once been a small chapel, Ceza decided; with skylights set into the small dome, it was something like an artist's studio.

Somewhat defensively Ceza said, "It's a beautiful room."

"You think so?" he said.

She perceived that things like rooms didn't matter to him.

"There's something I've always wanted to ask you —"

"What?"

"Don't be so impatient. How did you get your name?"

Stung, she said, "Ceza or Steele?"

"Ceza, of course."

"Caesarean section. It was my father's idea. That's how I was born."

"Well, I'm glad you were," he said. And took off his jacket.

She laughed and knew she'd been listening with her entire body.

"Another question. D'you mind?" he asked, with conspicuous tact.

"Certainly not."

"Are you initiated?"

"A little."

So it had happened easily — unspoilt — without virtue and without shamelessness.

And now she watched him and watched him as though she might never see him again, like this, with the small scar on his right cheek resting helplessly in that restless face, looked at his beard-stubble and wished she had a

90

magnifying glass the better to examine. She memorized the arrangement of his bones as she had his clothes. She needed to be aware of every bump, every impurity; and scarcely realized that she was mapping his moles and one or two blemishes on her own face. It was then his un-whiteness struck her again, and without pain. A non-Jew and a non-white... Incredible... Incredible... Well, there was nothing she could do about *that*. He'd turned her into a woman, and there was nothing she could do about *that*, either. Not now... not now... Her wrist was stiff with the watching weight of her head. And now he settled into his own sleep and held his head in a scaffold of both his hands; slim fingers laced his forehead and trussed the back of his skull.

She saw she'd been no more than curious about Paul — she could not now assemble his features in her mind. It was capricious of him to have faded so thoroughly, she thought, and indecent of her to have allowed it.

But Indra stirred.

Which wasn't enough to eclipse all of Paul.

Then he came awake. Quickly, and without the merest hint of having been asleep.

"My goodness, what time is it? I must have been asleep for ages. Now I'm late. We'd better hurry." He patted her thigh companionably, "You'd better get dressed."

She did as she was told without the least resentment, indeed, in a glitter of gratitude.

"I had an appointment with Mr. Cowley about my thesis. I think I'll make it, though. With just a little bit of luck. A little. Like you. You're more than a *little* initiated now, aren't you? Come on, tell me. Tell me."

"I'm almost a graduate."

"You'll have your doctorate before we're through." He patted her thigh again. "You must be starving. Next time I'll give you some food. I'll even let you see my kitchen."

Her honesty took her unawares: she said, "I can hardly wait."

Before they left he checked himself in the mirror. Ceza knew she would watch him do this many more times.

When they came together the next day he indicated where she should put her clothes, but only after he had shown her the kitchen. It was a small room, fragrant with a cinnamon-like spice instead of the curry she'd expected. She supposed she thought of cinnamon because that was how she saw his colour, as a confederacy of gold and cinnamon genes that had been collected from more than a thousand life-times for her. It was not yet the time for them to discuss the illegality of what they were doing and for the moment Ceza put aside all thoughts of prison. They would get to the mechanics of how the thing was to be arranged soon enough — he was probably expert at this, too: she was not — she was convinced — his first white girl, no, not by a long shot! At the moment, she was the subject of his excellence. It didn't matter that no end was or could be in sight: the beginning, rather, *the* beginning was enough — and he had severed the last edge of improbability.

They had almost the whole afternoon together. He gave her some granidilla juice, then invited her to take a shower with him.

"But my hair — ?" she said.

He laughed and the unpolished sound excused them

both, though she felt foolish. "My goodness," he said. "You can't be serious?"

"Well — it will show. It'll look odd. My mother will notice —"

"Oh, well — join me anyway —"

And so Ceza — who had become the servant of her surrender — went under the shower. Where desire mounted again.

Presently she said seriously, as if she were making a vow, "I'm going to invest in a shower cap."

"I think you should," Indra said.

She felt she'd been hugged.

Driving back to the university he said, "D'you think you could get to my place on your own tomorrow?"

"Yes."

He went on as if she'd said nothing. "You see, it won't do us any good if you're seen with me too often. You know that, don't you?"

"Yes."

"Discretion, as Molière has said, is always in season . . ." He added bitterly, "Why should we make it easier for them than it is already? The public library is two minutes away from my place. You can always go there. You ought to, anyway. That's where the reference library is. *I* can't use it, of course. Did you know that?"

"No."

"I thought not." He laughed briefly; the sound neither rose nor excused. "I take it you are not aware that one of the provinces in this country is like another country for me. I have to get something like a visa to get there —"

She sighed.

"Of course you're not culpable. It's not even your fault

that your hair can't take an ordinary soaking. With respect, we'll change all that."

Ceza bought a shower cap anyway. And found an obscure hairdresser to put matters right. Of course she telephoned to ask her mother to send the driver a little later. She would handle discretion with nothing but respect and compunction.

Dinner that night was as usual. Surprisingly, nothing at Villa Evermor had changed.

The silver bell, having sounded now as always, waited along with the scarlet-sashed waiter, Johannes, with the blue-black Jessica, purified grey evening apron, and Jacob, ready with his freshly picked vegetables, to chop the mint for the sauce. On one of the everyday, and therefore lesser, Madeira cloths, would be fruit in its inevitable Sèvres bowl. Philip Steele really believed that he had "no time for formality" because he would come to the table in summer wearing shorts and no shoes — and sometimes no shirt either.

Philip said, "You'll never guess who called on me today."

"Well, what could you do?" said Irene, indicating that she had already been told.

A sudden fear nagged at Ceza. Silence, measured by her rapid heartbeat, elongated. Had someone reported having seen her with Indra?

"Don't you want to know who it was?" Philip asked.

"Sorry, my mind was far away," Ceza said carefully.

"Sarah Goodman."

"Sarah Goodman?"

"She's a woman gone sour," Philip said dismissively. "She's started collecting for some charity or other. Can't remember which. Anyway, she wanted a donation, wanted the firm to take an advertisement."

"Did you give her anything?" Ceza asked.

"What else could I do? It cost me a small fortune. I took an expensive back page — some nonsensical programme —"

"How did she look?" Irene wondered.

"She looked as sour as ever," Philip said. "Paul's changed his mind, she said. He's now going to England to study paediatric neurology. She asked after you, Ceza. Said she was surprised you'd never contacted her. Hoped you'd nothing against *her* — That sort of thing."

"I should have phoned her — at least —" Ceza said miserably.

"You still can —" meditated Irene. "It's not too late. Perhaps?"

"But what could I say to her?" said Ceza, suddenly pessimistic.

"You could always tell her that you thought you didn't have what it takes to be a doctor's wife," Irene said over-earnestly. Her deep frown let Ceza know that this had been often and deeply considered. Irene had, as usual, chosen her moment. "You know, she probably felt worse than Paul. It's a terrible thing for a mother to have her son rejected. If I had a son I'd hate that, I know — she must resent *you*, too —"

In his most ominous tone Philip said, "Your mother's right."

Irene brought her hands in an attitude of prayer to her chin. She said, "It's silly and too easy to make enemies."

That settled things. Why invite the evil eye? Which was almost as dangerous as talking about *luck* . . . Ceza opted for the simplest. She said, "I'll phone her soon."

But was not altogether taken aback by the prospect of telephoning. It would be evaded, that was all. There might never have been a time when the Goodman family had crowded and stifled her mind. And yet Paul was, in some way, a remnant of the fraudulent past that Indra had made visible.

Paul's sluggishness could not now be refuted. For all that, she could not help knowing that she and Sarah had had something other (but what?) than Paul in common. . .

No, she would not telephone.

A certain insistence brought Ceza and Indra together every day. Ceza felt herself unravelling, then unravelled. Love had not been mentioned. She wondered at this, and understood how much of her energy had been consecrated to its avoidance; in spite of that underbelly so miraculously nerved, she'd let herself in for the kind nervelessness that put her out of touch with the whole notion of consequence.

There were mechanics, even so, to be worked out.

These, somehow, abridged time and encapsulated trust: a certain style of legality settled upon them. For another had to be told.

"D'you mind if I tell Neville Levin?" Indra said one day. The question surprised Ceza, but then everything he said, or left unsaid, astonished. Still she asked, "Why — ?"

"I'd like to see you at night. He could fetch you —"

"You trust him so much?"

"There are moments when one must —"

"Of course."

"Besides, who could be more suitable? You've said your parents wonder why you say at home at night so

96

much these days, haven't you? Neville's a qualified engineer as well as a final year medical student — perfection." He laughed briefly. "What do you think? Go on, tell me. Tell me!"

She said helplessly, "Has Neville done this sort of thing for you before?"

"Only when the girl was married."

Stricken, she said, "You *can't* mean it —"

He laughed again and she warmed to its sound the way she warmed to his voice, to the lilting accent which reached, she sometimes thought, the perfection of a lullaby. She outlasted her need to take his hand — his laugh, his laugh was enough. She said, "But won't it be an awful bother for him?"

"What — to fetch a pretty girl like you?" He added seriously, "No, Neville and I have been good friends for a long time. His mind is excellent. You must ask him, one day, what he has to say about medical school —"

"Ah, Indra, *you* tell me."

"Some other time —" He leaned over and, in a movement she had come to know so well and want so much, tugged her hair. "Come next to me," he said. "Next to me. Next to me."

"You know what?" she murmured into his throat, "My mother will like Neville Levin very much."

She held tight to his laugh and was not in the least let down.

So Neville Levin became a frequent visitor at Villa Evermor. In his mild grey eyes there lurked a faintly amused grin, a dark forelock spilled touchingly onto his forehead; his hearty weather-proof youthfulness was authenticated by excellent manners. Philip's notions of informality were not in the least disturbed by the way in which Neville addressed him as "sir." Neville had done very well academically, and insisted that it was all due to very hard work and "the reading of next year's text books this year." The Steele family delighted in his modesty. Ceza was never able to pinpoint how, or even when, Neville and Indra had become friends. And then, of course, there was Neville's altogether changed attitude — less a weakening than a rearrangement of his personality — whenever he was with Indra. Under the spell, as it were, of blatant admiration his admiration was inexhaustible; he never seemed quite at ease. And when he listened to Indra it was as if he longed to see as much as hear each word. His eyes took in Indra's every movement and Ceza felt herself disappear from his sight. Because Neville's adoration was in line with — and as mysterious as — her own.

Soon after Neville had seeped into her family, she'd begun to anticipate his asking her how she could have let herself in for such an affair, how she could have even thought of doing such a thing to her family. Later, when it became apparent that the question would never be asked, she knew it was because Neville saw her as the honoured one: any other way would have been as illogical as punishing innocence . . .

The first night Neville had fetched her had passed easily enough.

She said awkwardly, "It's very nice of you —"

"I have to go to the library anyway. Couldn't be more convenient."

"Isn't it terrible that *he* can't use it," she said.

"He has a photographic memory, you know," Neville said, appeasingly.

"I know, Indra's fantastic. I've even tested him — would you believe it?" she said making it clear that she wanted to talk about him.

"But how could you dare?"

"I don't know how I had the nerve. I simply asked him to tell me what he'd read while I checked. He even put the commas in."

The night that Neville first fetched her was the night that Indra gave her the sari. It lay on his bed in a shimmer of gold and emerald, and was the first thing she saw when, with even more than her usual nervousness, she entered. For a moment, because Indra was nowhere to be seen, she'd thought the sari belonged to an unexpected visitor and she'd known the unreasonableness of body-toothache.

"D'you like it?" he called out from the bathroom. "D'you like? Tell me — Tell me —"

"I've never seen anything so beautiful."

"Well, it's for you, and I'm going to teach you how to wear it myself!"

Wrapped in a towel, but still dripping, he came towards her, and Ceza, taken aback by his shape, said, "Oh, but the sari is not nearly as beautiful as you."

"Take your things off and we'll get you into this —"

But her hands fumbled.

He helped her and she was overcome with the gratitude she could not understand.

He tied a cord about her waist. Then she saw him make rapid pleating movements with the spread of gold and green silk. He let it fall back. He said, "An Indian woman is judged by the pleats of her sari. You didn't know that did you? You should have a petticoat, but this cord will do just as well. You see, you have to tuck it in—" He stood back to look at his handiwork. "My word, I've neglected the choli. Can't have bare breasts, can we? No matter how comely."

When at last he was done, he said, rather commanded, "Walk. Let me see how you walk. Walk to that mirror."

And she felt her walk change—touched by the skin-silk her legs seemed to take on the flexibility of arms while her back straightened. She said tentatively, "I feel graceful—"

He, meanwhile, studied her with an expression that leaned somewhere between astonishment and greed. "It's a very old sari," he said. "It belongs to my sister. Told her I needed it for a demonstration at university. So, of course, she gave me her best one. It was actually bought in India. My mother takes regular pilgrimages, a silk pilgrim. Anyway, this one is special because it comes from Benares. It was woven there, but with yarn that comes from Lyons."

Dazzled, she stared into the glittering mirror and saw the end of her transformations. She said shyly, "What a wonderful idea you had."

"Come here," he said. "And I'll show you a more radical idea." He thrust his fine-wristed hand into her skirt, untied the knotted cords, and unwrapped her. "We like unwrapping our women, you see."

Later he told her that he'd get hold of another sari which he would give to Neville. It would be kept in Neville's car, and she was to slip it over whatever she was wearing and cover her head with it so that she'd be less conspicuous at night. "You see," he ended grimly, "once we are breaking the law we might as well be professional about it. After all, don't forget — the penalty is usually six months' imprisonment without the option of a fine! So we mustn't be caught, must we? What d'you say?"

It was good that they could trust Neville, Ceza thought, if only because it was good that someone else *knew*... Her sense of privacy was in no way diluted — it had merely extended into a conspiracy of responsible silence. Besides, Neville's unquestioning acceptance added to a certain dimension of legality in opposing the law. When Neville did not come to fetch her it was because Indra could not see her. The Steele family understood Neville's absences very well — a final year medical student has to study. Neville had proved to be skilful at deception. He took Ceza to a family wedding where she was introduced to his mother.

Things would have to take their natural course, Irene decided, there was no point in rushing anything. Of that, at least, there was no doubt. Besides that, all was uncertain. True, Neville was too often at Villa Evermor to be only a casual friend of Ceza's. Besides, Ceza's excitement *before* she was to see Neville was definite — yet, when she was with him, there was about her a vagueness that perhaps discipline tagged to patience; it was the form of their open understanding that troubled Irene. Certainly Ceza spoke of Neville as often as she could have been expected to — her admiration, though nimble, seemed less than ultimate. Irene might have rushed things if she had not felt that avoidance of touch that cut the young couple into the kind of halves that are resoundingly complete. It was all as disconcerting as Ceza's overwhelming conscientiousness. Ceza was, after all, a student . . . Which did not mean that she should become a professor! All those books on politics and economics had kindled more than a flicker of panic that even those harmless, if rather stupid, books on child psychology could not placate. Those *political* books — weren't some of them banned — ? She would not ask. Nor think. Unformulated notions are more easily rejected: it was as if this instinct had been shaped by a thorough understanding of the value of ignorance.

Even in summer, when the grass was green you could still feel the bristly residue of the shortest winter. It pricked through Ceza's light blouse as she lay flat under the fruit trees. A pile of plums and figs, just picked, lay beside her. It was the end of the afternoon, when indolence is not only forgiven but expected. From under the trees even the sweet smell of rotting fruit seemed stationary, reminding Ceza of the fruity mist that penetrated Indra's room from the street of green-grocers below. Her head lay flat and seemed lower than the rest of her. She wished she had no clothes on, and of course that Indra . . . She was aware of grass in her hair, of small ants or other insects dawdling over her legs, of the pressing of the thick rooted arteries that sent up the strong blades of grass. Yes, she thought, Indra had taught her to see, and the more she noticed the more there was. Perhaps it was Indra's lightly sing-song accent which made her listen as carefully to tone as to content. Ceza was reading Bob de Jong's *Johannesburg Diary* in the early edition of *The Star*.

One of South Africa's "Little Men" who is getting bigger all the time is Mr. Philip Steele. Today the man who is both the founder and managing director of the Evermor Group announced that his chain of thirty-eight retail stores has just acquired Cosmos Dress (Pty) Ltd, and he is quite certain that his stores will serve as an effective outlet for Cosmos' entire production.

When I spoke to Mr. Steele about his latest coup (over the phone naturally, as he has no time for "wasteful business lunches") he said: "A mere ten years ago Evermor was no more (excuse the pun!) than a small suburban dress store started some years before by my mother. Shortly after taking the business over from her I saw the possibilities of expanding into the African market via a well-controlled credit system. I eventually hit on the right formula some five years ago and the group's growth speaks for itself. Since then, quite a few of the larger quoted retail groups have approached me to find out exactly how our credit system operates. And, naturally," he chuckled, "I've helped them wherever I could."

He went on to explain that the takeover resulted from a disagreement with the Cosmos Board and continued, "The present move is part of a continuing expansion and diversification programme which could well see Evermor become one of the country's largest unquoted groups. Our concern is with the future, not the present."

When asked about the financial arrangements of the deal, Mr. Steele, a rather humorous man, replied seriously, "The price is not for discussion and payment will be by cheque of course." Credit, apparently, is now a commodity Mr. Steele only offers!

Should he ever go public, this issue will be one of the most heavily over-subscribed of recent years.

She heard Jacob's whistling fiddle on the yawning air-lessness. Ceza wondered what Indra would say; he read the press with absolute thoroughness. Ceza's thoughts, as usual, sprang about. She was reminded of the much re-peated tale of her father's humiliation when he had come back from the war and his former employer had told him that he would only receive half the pay due to him, because a prisoner is not a soldier.

Irene joined her.

"I suppose you're half upset by the article," Ceza said.

"I'd have been happier if nothing had been printed. Dad's been working on this deal for ages."

"I know. We've actually discussed it while he's been helping me with my economics."

"But how is it you've become so interested in eco-nomics?" Irene asked unexpectedly. "I can't work it out. It's not that Neville is studying economics —" She floundered, but went on, "Not that what he thinks mat-ters too much to you — ?"

"Of course I care about what he thinks," Ceza rapped out. She added more patiently, as though she was think-ing out loud, "It's just that I'm not only interested in marks. If I was, I wouldn't have to work so hard. Mr. Cowley's never given me a decent mark, and God knows I work harder for him than for anyone else, and the others hand out A's so freely that they're meaningless." But it was Indra, Indra . . .

"I see," said Irene. "Mr. Cowley is about the only lecturer you ever speak of."

In her attempt to explain, Ceza sat up. Absently she pulled grass from her hair.

But Irene decided to change the subject. As if by way of a suggestion, she said, "Do you ever think of Paul?"

"Sometimes," said Ceza, who thought of him frequently, though always in relation to Indra. "I often surprise myself by thinking of him at the unlikeliest times." She stopped, but could not prevent the tell-tale smile that unlocked her lips. When she was wearing the sari, Indra had said, *"But it so becomes you,"* and wearing nothing he had said, *"But it so becomes you —"*

"Why do you ask? Why do you ask about Paul?"

"I saw someone who reminded me of him."

"But he's left. He's living in London, isn't he?"

"Yes. And when he's qualified he's going to settle in Israel."

"Really? I would never have believed that. But how do you know all that?"

"Sarah told Dad. She's been to see him again about another advertisement. Dad gave one to her, but not for Evermor. He asked her to make it anonymous, and gave it to her from his own pocket."

"Funny. I thought I saw her myself one day. Near the library. But I hope it was only my imagination."

"Well, your father thinks that Sarah only comes to see him about these advertisements and donations because she wants to have news of you!"

Ceza said, "Then I probably *did* see her."

"Of course she's curious about you," Irene said, "You jilted her son."

"I wish it had been the other way around."

"You probably wouldn't if it had been." Irene opened a fig, and put its strawberry-coloured flesh into her mouth. Ceza thought of *kum-kum.* Irene said, "Sarah's an odd woman. Sort of strange. I mean one would not have expected her to have carried on about a servant who had died. Look how she treats the living ones —"

"I know," Ceza said. She did not like talking about Sarah. She wished she'd never met her, never experienced that eternal reproach which had made her eyes into sockets. The merest suggestion of having seen her in Cross Street gnawed Ceza's eyes . . . Without meaning to, she said, "That woman frightens me — it's as though she's grown into —"

"But you must not think like that," Irene interrupted. "You've never done anything bad."

Things were getting out of hand, Ceza thought.

Neither Irene nor Philip was disposed to celebrate success (it would have been the same even if the announcement hadn't coincided with the fifteenth anniversary of Mrs. Steele's death).

However, they would not prevent the congratulations of others. The first of many phone calls was answered by Ceza.

She was unprepared.

That "Hullo, Ceza" was unmistakable.

"Mrs. Goodman."

"You used to call me Sarah, but never mind." The voice went on. "I phoned to congratulate your father. Wonderful news. Quite a coup, *n'est-ce pas?*"

"Thank you so much. It's very nice of you —"

"Well, I've been hoping to see you. Have a chat, you know. Actually I thought you'd contact me . . . But still . . . Why don't we meet for lunch one day — ?"

"It's kind of you to invite me —"

"Of course even busy students have to eat lunch, don't they? How about really good curry. You know there's that curry place near the library?"

"Yes, I know it —"

"Well, Ceza dear, you name the day —"

"Wednesday. How would next Wednesday suit you?"

"At about one o'clock. Excellent. And now, do you think I could have a word with that generous father of yours?"

Philip made short shrift of the call. Ceza's ashen face disturbed him. She, for her part, desperately did not want to spoil things, to cast a blight . . .

"What's the matter, my girl? It's only Sarah Goodman nagging me again," Philip said. "There'll be others, you'll see. None of them can stand it so they feel obliged to phone. *You* know how it is. But you look as if you've seen a ghost. You seem to be almost trembling."

Her laugh straggled to a quaver. "It's just that Mom and I were only just talking about her —" she managed.

"Telepathy then. So what? It's nothing."

"I know. We were just saying how odd she is. Now I have to meet her for lunch. I didn't know how to refuse."

"She told me about that. Also she said she was leaving it to me to see that you didn't put her off! Between you and me, what a mother-in-law you've escaped!" The phone was ringing again. "Ceza, I don't interfere in your life, as you know. But we've got a good understanding, you and I. So I'm asking you not to let me down. Not to put her off —"

"Of course I won't," Ceza said staunchly. But added, "You know me too well —"

"Better than I know myself, my girl, believe me —"

It seemed his cigarette, now at its end, would burn his lips. Ceza brushed the ash from his shirt automatically. And she leafed through the magic of believing every word he spoke. Her throat tightened. She said, "Quite right not to let them interview all of us."

107

Philip agreed. "I'm marking time," he said. "This is only the beginning."

It was the mention of a curry restaurant that haunted Ceza's waking moments and set her on the run from doubts strung from anticipation of lunch with Sarah. For surely Sarah could not *know*? Inconceivable. Yet even before the invitation she'd imagined a glimpse of Sarah in the ill-lit corridor outside Indra's very rooms. There was a pressure to tell Indra, to consult him. But secrecy was their imperative, as he'd made clear. And if he even thought that someone like Sarah had detected anything, he might feel constrained to . . . No, this she would not contemplate. Still, it was a secrecy beyond all laws of secrecy: Neville's inclusion only made things more — well, absolute. Indra had driven her to Cross Street no more than twice. They had not been seen together. Indeed, Indra had removed himself from the Student Council — not only that, but he was now only rarely seen in the student canteen. He'd excused himself from his former activities because he had too much to attend to with exams looming so close. He'd received the unprecedented permission to take his final law exam concurrently with the submission of his thesis for his Ph.D. The senate and council had approved this because academic freedom was drawing to its end and there was a move to appoint him to the university staff before this happened . . . No, it was best to say nothing of the impending lunch.

Still, the appointment with Sarah would be kept.

"You ought to wear a suit, Ceza," Irene said.

"Oh yes —"

"Maybe you'll phone me before your class? I'll be

dying to know what Sarah wanted. Just remember, she must have also been very hurt. An only child —"

"She didn't use to believe in any sort of ladies' committee work, you know," Ceza said, somewhat fretfully. "And now she's collecting for all these first nights —" She sighed. "What irritates me is that I'm going to have to miss a lecture. I was so taken aback when she asked me that I said one — I forgot the lecture doesn't end till one fifteen."

"Is it a very important one — ?"

"Yes," Ceza said shortly. She sensed Irene's impatience with her conscientiousness. Though Irene hinted obliquely, only.

"Would you like Joseph to fetch you?"

"Thanks. But the bus will be fine. I'll have plenty of time —"

"He's quite free, you know. That way you won't have to rush. Perhaps he could take you to the library afterwards?"

"I hadn't thought of that. Thanks a lot. Are you sure he'll be free?"

Ceza judged it wisest not only to agree but to appear attentive to detail. As if terror was being wrapped in a neat parcel with a fancy bow. Waiting, she decided, enlarges things. And if Sarah did know, what then? She would deny everything, no matter what . . .

As it turned out, Sarah kept her waiting. And all Ceza could do was trickle sugar in that half-empty grimy bowl. She need wait no longer than twenty-five minutes, she knew. And fifteen minutes had passed already. Hope was in each grain. She took in the detail of shape — perhaps Sarah would not come? Immersed in sugar, she did not notice Sarah's arrival.

"But what are you up to, *ma chère?*"

That confiding voice. Ceza winced all over, got to her feet at once and awkwardly. She said, "I didn't see you come—" She offered her hand, but had to wait once more, for Sarah was drawing off a fanatically white glove. Ceza's proffered hand dangled.

"Well, I must say, Ceza, it is good to see you again—" Sarah began. She glanced at her fingers. "Sticky," she said. "I can't think where I managed to get them so sticky."

"You're looking well," Ceza put in quickly. She looked about—a fly had settled on the bile-green wall behind Sarah. Which made Ceza add, "Do you often come here? It seems a very interesting place—" She broke off. An African waiter wearing a fez and long white robe was waiting for the order. Sarah busied herself with the opening of a small white *petit-point* case, and then extracted a lorgnette from which flowed a lengthy triple chain of gold. Curried lamb was decided. Ceza recalled Sarah's having been against restaurant curry. The little case was opened again. "What pretty glasses," Ceza said. "Could I see them before you put them away?"

"Yes. Arent' they—" said Sarah handing them over. "Very useful for programmes and menus, I find. Paul gave them to me before he left—" She'd been wiping her fingers and diamonds in swift polishing movements with one of those inevitable Swiss handkerchiefs of hers. "You don't go to concerts these days?" Her voice descended, "Paul gave us his season tickets. I've looked out for you but—"

"Oh no, I haven't been for ages," Ceza said sweetly. "And how is the advocate?"

"Working harder than ever now that —" But a sigh took over.

Her eyes were like dead roses, Ceza thought. And that narrow forehead of hers was so like Paul's, though she could not remember exactly what he had looked like, outside of photographs, that is. The woman's aged, Ceza thought. Her skin had gone scaly, as if with disuse. She asked agreeably, "How is Paul?"

Sarah's dead eyes looked merely dustier. "He's in London. But talks of going to the States. He's not specializing in gynaecology . . . You've heard — *n'est-ce pas?*"

Ceza shook her head.

The arrival of the curry could not have been more helpful. Ceza realized her hands had been sweating — it was good to smoothe them against the napkin. Nor was the curry any good at all, which pleased her, if only because she would never have used a ready-made curry powder, not now, not since Indra had shown her how to crush cardamom seeds.

After a while, Sarah said, "It *is* rather tough, this meat. I thought this restaurant was —"

Ceza speculated. She made a second reference to a reasonably avoidable question, and cut in, "I wondered why you'd chosen —"

"It was a silly idea. I hope you don't mind," the other's voice dipped confidingly, "— too much?"

"No, no. Of course not," Ceza rushed. "You said Paul might go to the States?"

"Yes. Paediatric neurology is his interest now — The States may be more advanced, you see —"

"Of course," Ceza murmured correctly.

111

"I suppose," Sarah said, "I suppose you're wondering why I asked you to lunch —"

"Well, I should have been to see you —" Ceza said miserably. "I meant to. But —"

"Yes. Well, I understand. Though —" She broke off and swatted after the fly that had moved from its perch behind her. That fly had been a teasing distraction to Ceza, though not an amusement. "I should be frank, I think," Sarah continued. "You see, although you were almost my daughter-in-law, I never got to know you very well. Oh, I liked you — but I didn't really know you. If you see what I mean — ?"

Ceza did not. She said, "I suppose that sort of relationship is —"

"Yes. Tricky," Sarah said firmly. "So I thought that we might now be friends."

"*That*," Ceza said feelingly, "is very kind of you —"

"It's good to keep in touch, you know. Now tell me about your life. University. I can hardly believe that I ever was a student there myself. Are you still interested in Native Law?"

"More than ever," Ceza said enthusiastically. "I seem to work hardest at that. We have an excellent lecturer. Mr. Cowley."

"Peter Cowley?"

"Yes."

"Didn't do very well in private practice, I'm afraid. Anyway, I'm told you see quite a lot of Neville Levin?"

Ceza laughed. She hoped, flippantly. "Quite a bit," she said.

"Not quite your type, though," Sarah said surprisingly, but sincerely. And more surprising still, "You know you remind me of myself."

For no reason that she could fathom (not even later and after much thought) Ceza said, "Do you ever hear from Whyte's family?"

"Not a word," Sarah said with her family aggrievedness. "We send money every month, but not a word."

"I'm sorry," Ceza said, meaning it. "My father told me all about the wonderful work you're doing —"

"At my time of life. A committee lady. Anyway, now that Paul and Doris are away it's a—" She stopped, making it obvious that she found these two absences more than she ought to have been called upon to bear.

Ceza said respectfully, "You know I'll have to think about going. In a few minutes. A lecture—"

"Certainly," Sarah said quickly. "I'll get the bill at once. *N'est-ce pas?*" She added, "A busy *complicated* girl like you. I've kept you too long —"

"Not at all," Ceza said awkwardly. "Not at all. It's very nice of you to have asked me—"

"Shall we skip the coffee?"

"I'm not in that much of a hurry!" Ceza said and laughed self-deprecatingly, which seemed safest. Her heart, though, had lurched so violently at the mention of "complicated" that she was sure it must have lumped against her blouse. In an effort to seem utterly frank, she said, "I'm glad you didn't go in for a post-mortem." And added quickly, "About Paul and me, I mean." Sarah, it seemed, was shaking. "I mean there would have been no point, would there?"

As if recalled, Sarah said, "There almost never is, in that sort of thing —"

"You see," Ceza said slowly, "You see *I* wasn't ready . . . A dreadful impediment I would have been —"

"My dear, I understand," the older woman said kindly.

113

"You were much too young. Paul will get over it, if he hasn't already. Men always do. Still, it will be nice to write and tell him that we met. One *must* be frank... You see, this thing caused a distance between Paul and me as well. We had been very close —" She shook her head. "Very close. But it's late and I've kept you too long, *n'est-ce pas?*"

They said goodbye on the pavement, with Joseph in full view. Ceza was aware of him, of his white drill coat, of his chauffeur's cap, of the sun, but most of all of the headache in which she felt she would surely drown. She sat beside Joseph, on the front seat, which was her only open way of defying the system. She'd asked Joseph not to wear his cap, *please,* but the man had stared at her uncomprehendingly, for he was proud of it, proud of being able to drive. She had a date with Indra after her class, but asked Joseph to take her straight home. She wanted her room, her mother's headache powders and the temporary oblivion of sleep. It was sticky in the car and difficult to hold her head up: she wished she could cradle it in her own arms, wished she could force it away from all thought forever. But facts and impressions whipped about her skull, and she held her hands against her ears to deafen herself to her mind. It didn't work: *What if Sarah did know —*? Ceza knew she could not predict Sarah's reaction... *would she tell her parents?* She groaned out loud.

"It's too hot for Miss Ceza," Joseph said.

She could barely nod. "Headache," she mumbled. And what would Indra say? She'd no way of letting Indra know she would not be turning up and this he would not take kindly — a headache would only irritate him. If only she could have talked to someone... Anyway, she would

114

tell her parents about the lunch, which was something of a relief. Because Sarah had changed. It was the kindness in Sarah's voice that was so upsetting — it did not match. But yet, she thought, moving her hands from her ears to her eyes, improbable as it had once seemed, it could be that something of Sarah was reflected in herself — an almost illegal need for secrecy, perhaps? Oh, God, could it be that each knew the other's secret . . . ? In a spurt of exhaustion she crashed her head against the car's window the better to stretch her body.

Once at home, she made her way to her bedroom but not before having asked Irene for headache powders and could she talk about lunch later, *please*.

Meanwhile, sleep . . .

To float freely into nothingness. To grasp mindlessness. But in the moments before this happened, Indra . . . And the woman that she became when she was with him, or alone with the sensation of him. That woman who both survived and defeated herself, who knew the sweetness of annihilation and the bitterness of resurrection as well a the devoted pain of ungodly belief. Ah, but her belief in Indra outstripped her religion: *her* god had a touchable pulse.

Her family, as it happened, felt instant sympathy for Sarah. The woman was lonely, it was good and kind and generous of her to want to keep contact with Ceza. Naturally, Ceza's lunch had been a painful experience, but life was like that, and, after all, she'd had the guts to go through with it. "Duty" as Philip said, "brings its own reward." Above all, she had not let her family down.

Yet Ceza was less tired than she had believed. For

when Neville phoned her, she agreed at once when he suggested fetching her.

And Indra's concern for her headache was as exalting as it was unexpected. He put her into her sari, he applied the *kum-kum,* and soon his feathery fine-wristed hands to her forehead. So that she found herself telling him about Sarah and the lunch — they even talked of Paul. And Indra's approach was like his touch, leafy and lilting so she confessed her suspicions. Which he banished. Their complicity was total and, *if* he loved her (he still had not said), it was for herself . . . Unqualified in the way of her family's and Paul's acceptance (Paul had become a cousin who'd outreached the proprieties, that was all) very few headaches were permitted and nothing but excellence was expected, Excellence was his natural standard — if she cooked or wrote an essay, or made love — her own excellence was exacted. And she'd not known she had any!

And all the while he stroked her head he talked to her of the insults, the failures, of the injustices, above all, the injustices he'd suffered, but not endured. And it was as if her entire body were compressed into that forehead: his fingertips might have been a breeze against it; because their lightness moulded and patted her mind — as if it had been a pastry — into his own shaping, his own design.

He'd restricted himself, he said, to university politics, had stayed among the educated, the enlightened, the truly free, and what was the use? Too many of them brought rattles to demonstrations. In the Great Hall, segregation despite all his efforts, segregation at university *social* functions, even a student light opera, so what was the use? The Prime Minister attacked the university because it had two hundred non-whites, out of a total

enrolment of four thousand — to be exact, 4,272 —
where was hope? He'd tried to organize a one-day strike
but it had been called off — and not by the authorities
but by the *students* . . . He'd addressed meetings, but had
been howled down with war cries — by students! And
this while he'd been bringing to the attention of the
student body that non-Europeans could not study physio-
therapy, could not study dentistry, because there were
insufficient lavatory facilities for non-white patients and
white patients were barred. Post-mortems on whites in
front of blacks were banned, too. But not the other way
round! And the irony of it was that black students actually had to leave the room during a white autopsy, but
the black cleaner, whose presence *was* permitted, staying
on and even sewed up the body! He would give her a
direct quote, he said; it was not something he had con-
jured up! "Native medical students must undertake that
at no time in their career will they treat Europeans but
this restriction should not apply to emergencies." And
the university authorities made statements about the
policy of the university being desegregated academically
but not, of course, socially. And this university called
itself an open university, while so-called teachers
preached student hyprocrisy and the fervent will to obey,
to submit... ! *How* could he stand it, to say nothing of
why? — Oh, he'd opted for the enlightened, naively,
because he had not known that the enlightened believed
that integrity went against self-interest. So they accepted, these enlightened students, that they were not to
wear their blazers or other identifiable university insignia
at political protest meetings — Why had there been no
ritual burning of blazers, *why*? No hope. Not by peaceful
means, anyway. Yes, it was true that he had been amongst

those who had successfully and peacefully cajoled the university authorities into readmitting twenty non-white medical students who'd been arbitrarily expelled, even though they had passed their exams and were already on their way. He'd felt, for a while, that it was worth a civilized fight — but now no more black medical students — even the trust fund that had collected R70,000 had had to close down. And the press published a letter wailing about the humiliation caused to a fine Christian lecturer at having an Indian girl fall in love with him — yes, yes, it was unbelievable, but Italian and Greek and other peasants were being imported as if they were vital medical supplies that could not be manufactured in South Africa! He was no Gandhi — he'd believed in educated planned disobedience and on all fronts the response had been pathetic. How could there be any possibility of any sort of justice at all, when those who were supposed to be emancipated, or liberal, or whatever other term one substituted for humanity, made no meaningful protest about segregated university tennis clubs or drama clubs or soccer clubs or even the odd dance. What a virtue was made over non-segregated toilets and canteens. Oh, he wasn't thinking of organized rebellion, that was like Ceza's long wait for the Messiah!

So make way for tribal universities. Meanwhile, read in your armchairs the written protests that have been sent from five continents and read the plaque that was going to be unveiled. He knew those ceremonial pretentious words by heart: "We are gathered here today to affirm in the name of the University of the Witwatersrand that it is our duty: To uphold the principle that a university is a place where men and women, without regard to race and colour, are welcome to join in the acquisition and advancement of knowledge; to continue faithfully to defend this ideal against all who have sought by legislative enactment to curtail the autonomy of this university... Now, therefore we dedicate ourselves to the maintenance of this ideal and to the restoration of the autonomy of our University." And Smuts, *Smuts* wrote the preamble to the United Nations charter. Which was about as meaningful as that plaque. What surprised him was that he was still capable of surprise. His guilt was the least forgivable of all — helpless hopelessness. Somehow, he'd have to redeem his self-respect, one day...

The anger had gone out of him, suddenly, and with it all energy. Only then did his fingertips abandon her tingling forehead. He'd been kneeling beside her but was now, sprawled, against the splintery floorboards like a collapsed cobweb. All Ceza's senses had been concentrated on his touch, on his voice, on the space between the words: the strain of grief, of indignation, of scorn and despair sped through words, through silences. Perhaps she could give him hope? Never had she felt closer to him! Something real, something active would have to be done, and with this decision the silence between them was, she fancied, musical.

So she watched him, saw his fine wrists gone tighter in clenched fists. She saw behind his eyes and deeper still: for she saw what lurked behind his nonchalance, and why he'd never spoken of love... That wrangling panic with his silence was drawn out as if it had been but a whim; his silence now cooled, and at the same time unsealed. *She would help.* Her every cell celebrated with intricate peace. Yes, she would help. At last, as if she could no longer remember herself, she whispered, "We'll think of something... We'll think of something —"

And that night their union undertook its final consummation — voluntary abstinence.

Security lay in resumption.

Later, while Neville was driving her home she asked, "But what exactly did Indra have to do with those medical students?"

"You mean those in my year?"

"I suppose so —"

"Without Indra they would not now be studying. One of them is said to be the brightest ever."

"Yes," she said impatiently. "But what did he do?"

"You mean he hasn't told you?"

"Never."

"That fits." He added mysteriously, "Now, at any rate."

"I don't understand," she said beseechingly.

"All that was during the Gandhi phase. When he believed in the triumph of one's own will, you know? That patient example was the only possible method to effect reform. In civil disobedience and non-co-operation, in solid and silent sacrifice. In picking up human excreta, if necessary. You know, the wholeness of life — all actions are linked, etcetera. He wrote brilliant letters on those students' behalf, he taught them how to negotiate with all the gentlemanly skill of a British diplomat. And he *was* successful, but only with those students. He'd hoped merit would be allowed to remain the only criterion. And then he discovered that the majority of those reprieved students were not interested in any other future students. If you ask me, he hates their apathy far more than the system —"

"And yet the system is responsible — ?"

"Not the way he sees it. Not altogether. The few interested are more concerned with mental exercise, you know, theoretical debate, than with anything else. You see, he thought he'd have an obvious chance with the educated — saw every educated person as liberal. It was his *sine qua non,* like forgiving the ignorant and the aged against whom discrimination is normal. As far as he is concerned, civil disobedience or passive resistance or *satyagraha* are now all out!"

"And you agree?"

"Of course. With Indra, you mean? Of course I agree!"

"Neville, may I ask you something?"

"I might not answer, but go ahead."

"How did you come to Indra?" When he did not answer, she found herself saying, "I don't mean to intrude — I mean, you're not obliged to reply."

"You know," Neville said thoughtfully, "I can barely remember not knowing him. He helped me once — I was, well, the truth is I was suicidal. He found me."

"You were — lucky —" (There, that word had been used and the car hadn't sundered. It was more than an omen, Ceza thought. It was a kind of purification.)

"I didn't think so at the time, but it was my lucky day. It was at the bottom of the grounds, near the rugby field. Carbon monoxide. It was past midnight. He found me and did the necessary to save my life, but it was his disgust that cured."

"I see."

"And I see you're too well bred to ask why I did it. So you won't have to ask him, I'll tell you myself. I was in love with someone. Not a girl either."

"How dreadful for you. And how lucky it was Indra."

121

"I wouldn't tell him about it, if I were you. If he'd wanted you to know, he'd have told you about it long ago."

"I'm sure you're right."

"And now it seems as if I can't remember not having known him. I ought to be frightened, I suppose, but there's no point." He sighed brilliantly. "What the hell," he said. "The guy purifies."

"I know," Ceza said.

But alone, in bed, her head still seasoned with his fingertips, she wondered. Because he had at last, confided in her. Because the tender tincture of restoration was in her hands. Because those breathstopping flashing moments of no lovemaking inflamed. He had almost come to rely on her; accordingly she extended her dependence on him.

And when they came together the next night there was no end to their meetings.

And soon he was telling her, "Did you know — did *you know* that non-whites like me are not allowed to possess a gun or any other lethal weapon? Even a blade over one inch long would be illegal in my unwhite hands."

"How would I know something like that?" It was so easy to tease, these days. "Whites like me don't have to know —"

"You're right. You're right," he said, letting delight flood the light of his face. "You're right —" He smiled mischievously. "Still I don't suppose you'd look after some tiny explosives that are *not* harmful." He pursued the emphasis, "Not harmful in the least. You wouldn't keep them, would you — would you?" His tone hit a near-whisper. "No. You wouldn't. I know you, I know you, don't think I don't —"

But in his cinnamon face his scar was a compelling flare. She longed to touch it, to put it out. She said "You see, you don't know me as well as you think! Of course I'd keep them! Why not? Couldn't be safer —" And she fingered the scar — hardly the sickle it had once resembled, it was now much more like a halved wreath.

"Well, you'd better hide it accurately. Well out of the path of all your servants. That stuff's lethal —"

"— Very lethal?" she said playfully.

6

It was the sort of Sunday family lunch — measureless and rumbling and thick with aunts, uncles and cousins — that had been going since the Steeles bought Villa Evermor.

The swimming pool bubbles soothed. Ceza felt, for once, a painfree lassitude — Indra's Hindu exoneration, perhaps? and absently tickled a fly from her arm.

Ceza stretched her slender body devoutly into the overwhelming sun, but still the whole sun seemed no less than refracted inner heat which edged and consecrated her own vivid privacy, a privacy which was no more expected by her than it was suspected by others. She would not call what she had a secret, for that would have subtracted from what she already understood to be profoundly scarce, but which, whether she was alone or with others, and even with Indra, endured — faithfully private and always a surprise. In a little while she would have to hand round the salads. And there would be even more than the usual variety today, Ceza knew, even if this lunch was only incidental to the series of pre-wedding meetings held for her cousin, Sally Lieb. Ceza knew better — at last, thanks to Indra — than to sit rigidly anticipating duties she never failed to discharge, and effortlessly pushed the salads from her mind without guilt. There was a time when the sun would have pushed *her* out, sent her into shadow with a sick headache, but that was before she had been shown it was possible to blast nerve endings. She looked at the bride-and-groom-to-be, for the hundredth time. Would they ever know each other's skins, ever pierce beneath? Ceza thought not. Sally Lieb as Sally Gordon, would change no more than her name. She had always been a *wifely* daughter! Sally looked at her Al with satisfied eyes, and in the way interest is connected to capital, his look combined with hers. How successful, their look said, to have done what had been planned for one, in giving pleasure instead of (the no less expected) sorrow to their joint parents. They sat in their bathing suits, his narrow arm draped over her anticipating shoulder, her left hand with its three-carat emerald-cut displayed with telling effect over his, as if they were already inside the gilt frames which would straddle the grand pianos of both parents. How alike they were — quite identical, Ceza thought. There was more than the same surgically chiselled noses, each mirrored the parents who were no more like impressions of what they had themselves to be; and in the general nature of things their taste could not but be monotheistic. Mildred Lieb therefore had the same frilled tulle toilet seat covers asBertha Gordon. They shared a great deal beside taste, of course — all would culminate: both families would unlatch and flood that special trust which over thirty years of close—but kinless—friendship had been held back. Ceza was aware that the marriage night, only two months away, would consummate more than flesh. Lieb wasin the property business and Gordon was in liquor, but they had recently bought a property in partnership with one another.

Philip, meanwhile, caught his daughter's eye. He raised his heavy reassuring index finger and shuffled his eyes in their recently prearranged signal, which meant: "Your wedding — and my son-in-law — will be just as good, if not better, my girl!" She smiled the conspiratorial and fully affectionate smile that he had always taken to be reserved for him. Her real privacy quickened then. A sigh seeped. Indra was unalterably Indian. She shut her flawlessly bright eyes against his non-existent white skin.

The occasional pitying glances, aligned to criticism, which her cousin, her aunt and Al's mother sent in her direction — because she was six months older than Sal and ought at least to have been pregnant by now — bothered her sensuality: if only they knew... But she had not been strong enough to be a bridesmaid. She had managed this by magnanimously giving her place to one of Al's relations, Cindy, by explaining with a rebuke she did not feel, but judged wise to imply, that Cindy didn't get nearly enough attention. And the family had to agree, and more, as Ceza had predicted, they could not but marvel at such a spectacular example of consideration. So she escaped the endless fittings, and had a sari instead. And proved, yet again, that nothing teaches the art of deception quite like the desire to please.

But the salads!

She left her pale yellow linen *chaise-longue* and slowly lifted the matching embroidered tulle which laid a veined membrane over fruit and vegetables teased and tickled into spirals, sickles, buds and bows. She stared at the meticulously accurate shapes as if for some clue — but to what? She was *of* them, she knew, having coiled cucumbers herself. Salads were, as Sarah had said, a Steele *specialité de maison,* and Ceza was reminded of a day at the university when a new friend had laughingly suggested that her home was probably crammed with doilies. Which she had emphatically denied. Yet she had failed *not* to think of salads . . . She felt guilty now, for even remembering. Consequently, when she began to proffer salads, she was truly penitent and at least as prodigal, with charm, but still extravagantly aware of her mother's appreciative glances.

It was clear, all the same, that her stomach could not cope with salad. It was as if it had become clumsy. The reeking heat of bees, of roses, of steaks, had made it so. She manoeuvred her plate away.

At last watermelons, shaped into tooth-edged baskets were served. The men split them, spitting black pips from competitive lips like bullets. Then it was time for them to "take a walk," as they put it, which meant that they favoured bushes over the poolhouse lavatory — despite its walls re-papered with newly valueless stock-certificates. Out of sight, because she was supposed to be supervising the servants, and forced to hide herself, Ceza demurely watched the sprays arch and cross. Then, because Indra expected her to, she eavesdropped:

"But Ben is so ill —" said Lieb, scandalized. "The boy's mad — he's got three children! He must be crazy." Aroused, as if at a personal affront, he declared, "What does he want to be — a martyr?" Then, with satisfied fervour — "He'll be back quick enough!"

A lazy considering smile was as near to a wince as Ceza could come. Israel, for her family was, she understood, that magical homeland it was unthinkable and unforgivable not to contribute to — yet heroic to visit: they would be buried, even so, with their heads immemorially turned towards it — but how could it be called a real homeland when it could never be as good for the Jews as South Africa had been — ?

"I don't know about Ben Rosenberg being ill —" said Gordon. He added wisely, "But I do know they're in trouble."

"What's gone wrong?"

In his stout style of logical disparagement, Gordon murmured: "Bad management. Isn't that usually the trouble? That son of Ben's is mad on golf."

"So they'll settle ten shillings in the pound. So what? Their creditors will take losses and give them credit again. You think it hasn't happened to me — as a creditor? Money's tight, that's also the problem," said Gordon, shrugging his lips.

"But the Rosenberg business has been on top for years," said young Al, most pensive with excitement. "I remember when we battled for their account, hey, Pop?" His father's neck buckled agreement.

Reassured, the son flung on, "But they can't be thinking of letting a business like that go! I don't think one of our delivery boys hasn't bought a bit of crappy Rosenberg furniture at some time of his life."

His sense of arithmetic, swift, boundless and always close, tightened his eyes.

"Sounds like something we'll look into," he remarked, with just the right mixture of dubious yet thorough appraisal that hinted of another merger in the offing.

Forced to admire, Philip said: "A son-in-law like you, that's what I'd like." And why should he not speak

129

his mind, even though his wife Irene would have disapproved?

At the mention of son-in-law, Ceza, by way of argument, smarted avidly.

It was conversations like these, she told herself, which seamed more tightly their thick cord of common purpose, and kept them well sealed from boredom; more importantly, this kind of gossip supplied those indispensable nuances that instructed their decisions, and although she saw the cord as belonging to *them,* she was half-aware of being safely looped to it, too. The thought left her unaccountably irritable and at once and expertly she set about disguising it from everyone, especially herself.

And when, still smarting, she rejoined the women, she found them as she had left them, prodigiously bent over the hot woollen colours of their embroidery.

"Here, darling," her mother said, rippling her wrists as if to rinse heat. "Try some of this solidified cologne against your forehead. There," she said as soon as she had anointed Ceza, "that looks better. You feel cooler now. Al's mother just made me a present."

Ceza murmured, "So cooling."

But her forehead felt overturned.

In the stationary heat, needles hovered.

"Honestly, it's just like that *Chamsin,*" said Al's mother, still silted up from a recent visit to Israel. "You like the cologne, Ceza? I brought one for you, too."

"How kind of you. Thanks Mrs. Gordon — Aunt Bertha."

"That's better. We're all one family now —" Aunt Bertha said, and looked towards Sally's small breasts that would soon spill the news that would make them truly one family, one selfless family. She'd already worked out the announcement: "To Alan and Sally (née Lieb) a son, Arthur." Called after her own father, Abraham, just like Al had been. "First grandchild for Bertha and Dave Gordon, and for Ruth and Natie Lieb." At this her own unbanishable breasts felt heavier, as if they held the rush of milk that was waiting for Al's son. A good omen, but to make sure, she banged her elbows against her bamboo chair.

"You know, Mom," Ceza asked tentatively, "I have to excuse myself. That essay —"

"Of course, darling," Irene said. But smiled conspiratorially. She once again found herself remarking, "Ceza takes her education too seriously . . ." Then almost appeasingly, she added . . . "her father's fault for having told her to do her best." And with a fluttery bonding laugh — "But he gets a kick out of helping her with her economics. Of all the things in the world it has to be economics!"

"She'll be studying Doctor Spock soon enough," Al's mother said. "There's nothing to worry about." She laughed too comfortingly.

Irene thought it best to join her. Those helpless doubts of hers fell within the folds of her perpetually changing daydream of Ceza's tulle wedding dress; yes, the wedding would simply have to be on the lawns. Irene's impatient fingers, reinforcing a decision made when Villa Evermor had been bought, dismissed Sal's tapestry. Her gaze travelled her exorbitantly irrigated, though never really green lawns, through the windows to the duck pond in which they kept carp, then back again to the sunken garden in which they kept more than a thousand rose trees. But where to place Ceza's wedding tent? Would they really have to do away with some of the yellow roses? Helpless, as always, before too many choices, she twitched her gaze to the others and said, "I was thinking about the wedding."

Irene's tone was perhaps too rapturous; reminiscent, even.

Sal's mother said sharply, "But what else? Did you *hear* us when we said we've already got seven chair backs done?" And flourished her tapestry with annoyance.

Irene blinked at the tapestry as if at a searchlight.

"Ceza's almost finished the one she's doing for Sally —" she began dubiously. She began again: "Ceza simply *makes* the time —" but was silenced mercifully, if automatically, by one of her new gardeners who was gliding across the lawn with a tray of fruit juices. He was about Ceza's age, but looked younger; his skin seemed freshly black; he whistled a humorous half-sad piccaninny's tune, and his muscles, behind their white drill, played energetically — as if to glean even more heat.

Ablaze with graciousness, Irene said, rather, gasped, "Just what we needed, Job! We've all been nearly dying — How did you know?"

"Miss Ceza, she tell me to make a tray, ma'am," Job said. His short and shy laugh permitted a glimpse of strong white teeth, — each one a vivid flag of obedience. "I can make some more, Ma'am?"

He went off, whistling, and if his whistling had been shrugged into another key, they did not notice. The difference was keyed to his own kind, anyway.

And upstairs in her room Ceza, who knew nothing about Job but his first name, felt for no reason that she could name, that the whistling was aimed at her. But gently. . . . She listened until it was over. Then she took the white coverlet — crocheted by Jessica, from her bed. She preferred to ead in a sprawl. She liked her room but had never turned to it for comfort, though it was cool, and its pinks soothed. Beside her bed were the red roses Indra had sent, but which had even been ordered from the florist by Neville. She reassured herself: Irene and Philip approved more and more — how could they not? — Neville was loaded with nothing but the most permissible blood. Still, if Ceza had not turned to the powdered silence and timelessness of her room for comfort it was only because she had never been in need. Lately, however, she had taken to using her room for what she thought of as — well, thinking. . . . Yet, perhaps she received some sort of strength from the wedding cake pinks that hung, still as cake-icing, in the tulle skirt of her bed, but fussed in a flurry whenever she drew the pink mosquito net from the shellpink ceiling. And if it was not comfort, as Ceza was sure it was not, then it was a complicity of nothing but silence. The sort of silence which would allow her to hear, sometimes — inside the corpuscles of all the family-love which circulated through her — the prance of her own heartbeat? Or it may have been no more than the room with its infant pinks unborrowed from the childhood her mother never had. For all its babyishness was somehow redeemed from fluff, and was, instead, charming, and more — for there, again and again, as Ceza had tested, virginity could be magically repaired and perpetuated. And then again, because her room was something of a sanctuary, like an underground bunker, it was an excellent cache, for explosives . . .

A bird stirred the ivy against her window, and from the servants' quarters she heard the sound of a cunningly strummed guitar.

Now her forehead was in place; tenderly she fingered its centre — tonight Indra would carmen it, and then she'd be a Hindu girl. *And then . . .* ! And who on earth, however deeply their looks might search, could guess — viewing that abstract water-colour prettiness of hers, that unafraid though scarcely confident expression that mixed so well with the gravity of her mouth — at that privacy which her skin knew, sheltered and distilled.

It was her skin, turned by Indra into insect's feelers, which had scented out that the world was not an uneven split between too few Jews who were also non-Christians, and Christians! Again, she ached to say, "Indra, Indra — I'm going to call you 'I' for Indra, and 'I' for me."

Yet she had not done this. As much as she longed for a solid, formal expression of intimacy, her awe of him acted as an elision, she did not have to be told that any kind of endearment, no matter how privately uttered, would have seemed too public, and almost defiant. Even now.

She prepared her bath — for Indra — with scent and oil, and when it was ready she decided to read her essay again. The essay, entitled "A Redefinition of Prejudice," was more comprehensive than she'd hoped, thanks to the attentions of Indra's concise legal mind. He'd taught her how to work. And when she'd believed she must be like most of the others who placed all the emphasis on getting away with things, on minimal effort, he'd shown her that she actually wanted, and even had a need, to learn. She'd become, she supposed, a serious student, and this half dismayed her, though like a shadow in a dream, it was not something she talked about. An education, her parents had said. Any kind of education you like, and one day even Oxford or Cambridge. But it had all been said, though not deliberately, as if it were the kind of fantasy best left unrealized. They really meant — and this Ceza understood and accepted in much the same spirit of tenderness with which they regarded her — go to university as long as you don't take it seriously. *They* had not managed to complete high school. Their regret at not having had the opportunity was real enough, though somewhat offset by Philip's uneducated chain-store success. The opportunity to choose, they continuously let her know, had been hers — and because the *choice* had been unimportant, she took Social Science if only because the central thing was that here, in South Africa, their alien illicit skins had been unpeeled, and with them university quotas. But Ceza still felt her skin illicit, and so united with Indra's . . .

True, her parents had given her everything, and even trust, because in the end, and before long, she'd be a wife and mother, and inside the real phase of her destiny.

But now her parents were — impossibly, it seemed — excluded . . . The continuing newness of that privacy of hers, so precious, so scarce, was something like an illegitimate foetus, integral yet separate. She seized her parents' miraculous ignorance as some kind of guarantee against the Immorality Act — what was the secret police compared to parents who knew you better than you knew yourself?

These thoughts appeared to thump her skull with all the familiarity of Mendelssohn's wedding march. She pinned her hair away from her face before climbing into the bath. Then she remembered Sally's tapestry. The tub was deep and wide, yet she managed to get out of it very quickly, and only returned when she fetched the tapestry, which she proceeded to sew furiously, in time with her thoughts, whilst, with deft flicks of her toes, she added more and more scalding water. She sewed busily. After a time, about fifteen minutes, she became aware of the over-softening of the pads of her feet, of her heels, and dropped the sewing to the floor. Then she spread the skin slivers along her wrists and examined the tread, those fine lines which unfailingly reminded her of Indra's overworked eyelids. How easily, she thought, skin comes away — what a surface thing it is anyway, and the concept, already constant, was as forceful as a new vow. It was too hot, and she felt the sweat gutter her skin. It was time to leave the bath; the family must be waiting for tea. She veiled herself in talcum and the trails of powder, of towels, of underwear, bottletops and hair were as good as invisible because Jessica saw to all of that. Meanwhile, she reiterated her resolve that she would learn how to iron, to wash her own underwear, at least, for herself — and Jessica, of course, would delightedly leave anything, even the oven, to teach her. Of course she cooked in Indra's crude kitchen, and cooked well. But the most delicious ingredient was that she could no more believe this than Jessica would have done! It was all part of her privacy, her secret, as if the unbelievable were the essence from which secrets are distilled.

Now Ceza selected the silk beige skirt and blouse her mother thought suited her best; just the right thing to wear tonight for her ostensible date with Neville Levin. (Once in Indra's rooms, if she wore anything at all, it would be a sari.) She picked up Sal's tapestry and carefully appraised it, it could not be faulted: it was like her essay and she looked forward to the family's praise no less than to an "A," and the pencilled congratulatory comment.

At the poolhouse needles still hovered in the sun like firefly wings, the filtration murmured, Philip's scar was now dulled by his sun-reddened skin and the bridal couple still sat inside their gilt frame — a little more puffily perhaps. The combined families were by this time thoroughly agreed on how they would acquire the Rosenberg business — it was as good as done. She held the tapestry out for their inspection, for their comment, as if it were a road map or a platter of complicated salads she might have designed herself... Praise, as she knew, pleased more deeply when it was deserved, and under the bright breathlessness of Irene's fullest approval, it was perfectly impaled. Once again she had proved her devotion. As if proof dominated truth.

Paul's was the only room in which Sarah and Whyte had not held one of their conversations: now that neither Paul nor Whyte was part of the household, Sarah found that room least hurtful, a comfort if anything. It contained so little of Paul, so little that was familiar to her. He'd left most of his medical books, had given away the clothes he didn't need. The cupboards were empty, the walls were covered with anatomical diagrams, the sticky tape which attached them had gone sallow and dirty, like stained fly papers. She was as indifferent to them as to the kitchen whose deep-freeze now stood unlocked and empty, oozing a ripe smell of decay gone sour. You could have found Paul's desk in any office: there was nothing distinctive about it, which was fitting, Sarah thought. She'd resigned from all her committees, and now only used the desk when she wrote to Paul. Each weekly letter was a matter that drew all energy from the following week. There was so little to say. . . . Besides, as Sarah knew it, they'd degenerated into two strangers exchanging polite notes of thanks across an ocean. His weekly envelope had come to signify a tiresome reply — like those phone numbers that the incorrigibly dirty Judith wrote on an old envelope which meant nothing more interesting than a telephone call to an electrician. Even if she had had all sorts of things to write to Paul about, the letters would have been a trial — she now felt obliged to check the spelling that had once been perfect, and was compelled to rely on a little pocket dictionary — undersized — the kind she used to despise. The real dictionaries were in Louis' study and she only entered that room when she was forced to. After all — it had to be faced — what was there that she could actually say to Paul? Could she tell him that the life she'd never had was flooding out of her? But today she had news, she would tell him of her lunch with Ceza, but would be careful not to permit him the smallest chance of guessing that all that was left of her enthusiasm was impaled in Ceza. Because he'd been insatiably close to Ceza; it could have been any girl, but it was Ceza who had been his mother's stand-in.

She began:

Paul, my dear,

It was good to have your letter. I can't begin to imagine the cold in London, have never been there at this time of the year, as you know. But is your coat warm enough? Glad your throat is better. Take care, I hear that 'flu in England is a very different thing from 'flu over here. Of course you will be better off when you have your own apartment — you were not made for landladies, *n'est-ce pas*?

ut won't that be difficult to serve? To eight hundred
le?"

es. It will be quite a thing. But they're having
n waiters—"

re they better?"

h, yes. Much more efficient. Always have been—"

ore experienced, I suppose," said Ceza.

l's changed her bridesmaid scheme. This is the
change. From pink to navy blue to mauve and
checks—" Irene tried to sound irritated, but
. "Such a scene at the dressmaker's today. Sal in
nd M. Rampon in hysterics. Anyway, mauve and
checks. That's the theme. Mauve and white flowers
blecloths—"

a said, "I don't believe it." She added derisively,
't it clash with the pink champagne?" For she
hear Indra's future laughter; the projected sound
er flush.

n't be such a snob, Ceza," Irene said in one of her
t firm tones of sparkling disapproval.

on't mean to be a snob," Ceza said, immediately
etic. "It's just that it all sounds rather much."

a's right," Philip said disgustedly. "It's disgust-
stentatious."

they're having those cabinet ministers. It has to
ial," Irene said defensively.

t's why they should exhibit some taste," Philip
ly. "Between you and me, that's precisely why."

lra, when he was told, did not laugh. That was his
ue, Ceza decided, not to do what she'd expected.
l, "I feel for you—such vulgarity does not
you, not at all. It does you injury. It reminds me

142

Life goes on. Your father is well, but working too
hard, as usual. Some huge and boring fraud case I
think. We don't know the people—they seem to be
among the silent millionaire group. Anyway, your
father is intrigued—he may have to go to New York.
If he did he could meet up with your Aunt Doris and
Uncle Dave. Have had about four post cards from her
this week, so it looks as though she is missing her
older sister. They're all having a great time. Keep
receiving things from her for her—all marked "unso-
licited gift." I can't imagine where she'll put them all
when she gets back! Six beaded bags at least—all
cluttering my cupboards. I may have to use your room
if things keep on at this rate! Judith or I drag all the
way into town every few days collecting the set of
Venetian glass she's sent herself. On top of it all
they're garish green—my *bête noire*—

Philip Steele has done some grand deal. I forgot to
enclose the newspaper cuttings with my last letter. I
phoned him (I had to, you know how generous he's
been with all my charities!). Irene and Ceza seemed
pleased to hear from me and the upshot of it all was
that Ceza and I had lunch together. She asked after
you—most keenly, I must say. She looked tired, but
still pretty. Says she's working very hard. It seems she
has the greatest admiration (one your father does not
share) for a man called Cowley. Anyway, I'm telling
you about her because she *so* distinctly asked to be
remembered to you. Also, to be frank, I find it necessary to point out that if you were hurt—what's the
use of pretending? the injury was more in the ego than
in the soul.

139

So you see — your mother has been thinking of all sorts of strange things, like hearts — and if you think this is not quite my line, I can't blame you — !

My experience is almost entirely limited to un-broken — and therefore redundant — hearts.

A mother should not mistake her son's stomach for his heart.

Write soon — we can't help longing for your letters.
Love, Mom.

Judith was usually summoned as soon as Paul's letter was done — but today Sarah hesitated.

She considered Paul's handwriting again — it had always lacked energy. She was aware of always having examined him for faults, for flaws, but only to pluck them out, like ticks from a poodle. A poodle might help, she thought. What was that dog's name — the one they'd had in the old house? She could not remember. Yes, she just might acquire another poodle. She could call it Ceza, or something like that. Ceza would have been a good name for a poodle, anyway... Ah, yes, now that she'd taken Ceza to lunch, she was relatively sure about her. That glow — surely Irene could see! It was the sort of light that bit... She would have to find out, leave no room for doubt. And then? And if? Who cared, it was the knowing that mattered. An absolute sigh all but snuffed her being. Had it been possible to like Paul, she would have not had to adore him.

Indra's interest in the coming wedding seemed insatiable. Ceza found herself telling him again and again who would be there, what menu variations there were, which non-stop bands were to play, how the fountains were to

140

be installed. For the Liebs had been comp
City Hall. That was where they held the
certs, wasn't it? He, of course, had never
go. Still, he knew the City Hall anyway
enough tame political protests there, had

"Perhaps if I got myself dressed up as
I could get in. That way I could see you.
Indian waiters, aren't they? They usually
are so posh, don't they?"

"I forgot to ask. But you're probably
"Well, find out will you? Find out.
this and I'll tell you why when we kn
waiter they've selected."

"Yes."

"But be discreet. Discreet. Rememb
be obvious —"

"Oh — Indra —"

Her mission was accomplished easil
now only four weeks away, was cor
about — indeed, its impact seemed e
Philip's new deal.

Dinner was the ideal moment.

"Have they reached agreement on t
asked her mother while she held her fat
been some inter-family friction about
Philip shared a private amusement.

"Mauve and gold printed on wh
quickly.

"That sounds unusual. But I meant t
"It's still between filet mignon and
said doubtfully. "Philip, don't encou
We'll have to face these sorts of decisi
day."

141

of my mother's silk pilgrimages."

She felt tranquil. But expectant nevertheless.

"Come next to me," he said patting his thigh. "Next to me. Next to me."

Ah, she knew what that meant.

And it was over unusually quickly; and it was as if speed were equal to strength, for she could not recall any time like it. But for Indra it was only a temporary interruption inside their conversation. He began to talk at once and seemed oblivious to Ceza's exhausted dreamy responses. She did not wish to recover, had no intention of listening, and lay back in the chair, restfully swinging her ankle. But soon her fingers found the hooks of her choli which they undid, found the string which held the dishevelled pleats of her sari, and removed them, daintily; her ankles rocked restlessly. She had never before been so forward; the initiative always came from him, as it had from Paul, and in the sudden freedom of exhibiting herself, her ankle shivered.

He no sooner heard than saw.

"You're a greedy girl," he said. "Greedy. Greedy."

She'd been turned into a knowing tic: she'd been split, and split again, until it seemed she was no larger than the space between her eyelid and eyebrow.

The alarm went off as usual, ten minutes before Neville's arrival. No sound penetrated those two unconscious bodies. So Neville had to rattle the door handle. Ceza heard and roused Indra while she scurried to the bathroom. Indra did not, could not, bother to dress. His nakedness made Neville blink.

"I hope no one saw anything," Neville said. "I had the feeling someone was in the passage."

"Take off your fez. It doesn't suit you. Though you

look Moslem enough. That olive skin of yours has prodigious uses." Meanwhile he slowly, and perhaps rather too obviously, went about the collection of Ceza's clothes. "I'm bringing your things," he called. "*What* a hellcat —" he murmured to Neville. "Took me unawares —"

Neville looked away. He said, "Hadn't you better get dressed?"

"I'll do that," Indra said. "Look, Neville, could you come back after you've dropped Ceza in the safe confines of Villa Evermor? I think the plan's been formed — a matter of self-evolution I'd say."

Neville jerked his head in the direction of the bathroom door. "Does she know?" he said.

"Not yet. Not yet. But she'll be told in due course. The whole thing is hinged on her —"

Later, beside a traffic light, Neville said: "I think you'd better clean yourself up —"

She turned sharply toward him. But the glory in her body left her hurt-proof.

Still, when they were inside her driveway, she said, "You needn't see me to the front door, you know."

His laugh offered friendship again. "Oh, but I must. Besides, what would Indra say?"

The dining-room light appeared to be on. She went in to investigate and found that one of the Sabbath light candles had fallen against one of their best embroidered cloths. "It must have only just happened," she thought, as she efficiently put out the still mild flames. "Of course, it's Friday night. Though how could I, tonight, differentiate nights?" She almost giggled. She hoped Irene would not come in for one of their chats. But Irene had been waiting. "Oh, Mom, I'm so tired tonight.

Please. I don't want to hurt you. I can't think of anything but sleep. *Please . . .*"

"Of course, darling." Ceza felt lips that were too dry against her forehead.

The underside of Irene's consciousness that had begun to suspect some kind of family withdrawal in Ceza's attitude was more than assuaged by her daughter's wholehearted interest in the Lieb wedding. For Ceza's curiosity was, in the circumstances, more than touching: from their earliest childhood Ceza and Sal had taken it for granted that Ceza would be the first to marry. Irene had come to believe that Ceza regretted her decision over Paul — why else would she bother with Sarah? Since that lunch the two of them had even met for tea . . . And if Ceza was still in love (as Irene thought of it) with Paul, then she was wise and brimming with femininity in preserving and consolidating her relationship with his mother. The poor child had even stopped confiding in her own mother just to save her from anxiety, which, Irene fretted, was all very well, but what were mothers for? It was, well — delicate. On the other hand, if she and Neville were good friends (how she loathed the whole idea of good friends!) why was Ceza so desperately tired, almost irritable, after a night out with him? *Children . . . !*

Well, she was good at waiting, at choosing moments — didn't she advise Philip in his complicated negotiations which were really no more complex than women's instincts which were in turn connected to those natural or bodily mechanisms (if what is bodily is also natural?) that so well understood the intimate art of timing?

By now it was mid-October, and meant to be spring,

but summer, it seemed, had taken over in advance of its time: the buds were like precocious adolescents and became full and ripened too soon—it was as if withering and dying would come ahead of time, too. And at the university, the students bent under the weights of their books, the libraries, usually empty, were suddenly cluttered with students who wilted and crushed like too many staling blooms on a single branch. Nails were bitten, hair straggled in greasy streaks: all was rush and alarm and guilt. Even the most ordinary gardens were feverish with colour—but lawns were dry, the country prayed for rain, and was saluted by a sun which marched ever-widening skies. And jasmine and wisteria spread everywhere but at the university, which seemed forever determined to guard its bare bricks, and barer concrete.

At the Lieb household the heat seemed inappropriate; the family had taken to using Irene's headache powders. There the rooms were crammed with too many roses, too much fruit lay wilting in too many bowls. The study had been cleared to house wedding gifts, more tables had had to be brought in—though the wedding was still three weeks away: it had been necessary to bring in more tables. These tables, needless to say, were covered with mauve and white checked cloths, and the servants brought in fresh vases of mauves daily. Japanese iris and dahlias and even water lilies were plucked from ponds at day-break—a novel idea which pleased Sal enormously. Guests who came to view soon caught onto the idea, and mauve dinner services, teasets, and even glasses began to be unpacked, all to be carefully entered on mauve pages under the mauve and white checked covers of the book that Sal had made herself. Soon shelves were freed of books, to accommodate useless ornaments, breakfast sets and a priceless stock of mauve Venetian vases and ashtrays.

Irene had feared that Ceza might display that sort of snobbery which was so dismaying. The Liebs might have felt that Ceza mocked Sal, that going to university (exactly as they had predicted) had made Ceza uppity, "too big for her boots." They may well have been right, Irene supposed; but for studying — pointlessly — Ceza and Paul would have been married. But Ceza's exemplary behaviour was a rebuke in itself — when had Ceza ever let her down? Except for Paul, perhaps — but here Irene's feelings were too delicate, and perhaps — petulant — ? to withstand probing. Besides, Ceza would ultimately become Mrs. Paul Goodman, the physical thing that Ceza had spoken about would (in the end result) be handled in the way nature had ordained. Not that Ceza was being contrary — diffident, certainly, though far from helpless. Just look at how she had entered into the spirit of Sal's wedding!

But the latitude of Ceza's enthusiasm was more — well — diligent than it needed to be. For, of all things, she wanted to know what arrangements were being made for Jessica, Jacob, Joseph and the others to attend the wedding. Ceza, it seemed, had taken their inclusion for granted. Worse still — the Lieb and the Gordon servants would have to attend, too. Nor was she shy about expressing these views to Sal. Their exchange had been almost acrimonious, and in the end Ceza had insisted that she, for one, would not go unless these *people* who worked devotedly for the Liebs and the Steeles could at least attend the synagogue. Naturally the marriage families chose to interpret this as jealousy revealed, at last. So out of an altogether agreeable sense of pity properly distributed with remarks on Ceza's craziness, they gave way.

"But why?" said Indra when she reported this latest event to him, "Why did you let them know you even know of the existence of the underdog — leave alone — care? Or has the fact that they're merely servants escaped your tiny mind? Attention has been inauspiciously drawn to you. Inauspicious indeed."

"I'm sorry." She brightened and added, "But they all know how much I adore Jessica. It's almost a family joke—"

"So I would imagine," he said bitterly. But sounded sanctimonious. He added, "I am under no misapprehension concerning the way you people think—"

"That's unfair—"

"How so?"

"What about you and me?"

"Well—?"

"Indra—Oh, Indra—" Though shorter, because since Indra and Mr. Cowley she'd given up varnish, her nails still pierced her palms; that intelligent girls did not cry was one of his more ardent tenets.

"You greedy thing — I was merely testing!"

His perfectly balanced laugh let her draw breath.

"Testing," he said again. "Merely testing. And you did not cry and I'm proud of you. I love your greed, you know." Then he scowled disgustedly. "Just listen to that," he said. "Listen."

She understood that she'd been oblivious to the sustained weeping that issued from the flat next door — she'd become so used to it that it was now no more interesting than refrigerator sounds.

"Why does she cry, Indra? D'you know?"

"She is barren and her husband is about to divorce her —"

She shuddered. "I see," she said.

"But you're not. You're too greedy. I can imagine how many babies you'll have one day!"

You, not us, thought Ceza. But she lied flippantly, "I've never even thought of babies."

Suddenly, as if pursued by his own energy, he paced the room. "How will I pass as a waiter? Sometimes, even for menial work, it's not enough to be Indian —" He wheeled about, "What, might I ask, are they wearing?"

"Who?"

"The waiters, you silly greedy thing —"

Suitably contrite, she said, "I could find out —"

"But tactfully. Discreetly. I always feel obliged to remind you of elementary principles, don't I?" He repeated, satisfied, "Don't I? Contrary to principle, I feel responsbile for you. You must contrive to assume responsibility, to assume consequence."

A wince tugged her bowel. She did not feel entirely foolish, but unsure, and, always (except for lovemaking and sometimes even then) inexpressibly unequal. He offended easily, though not, she knew, unintentionally. A sadness. But then she noticed his violet shadows looking dirty and a rush of tenderness and culpability came to her lips in an awkward laugh. She said tentatively, "I think I've thought of something —"

His shoulders swooped forward. "What's that?" he said agitatedly. "What could you have thought of?"

"It's only an idea —" she began excusingly. "I haven't thought it out —"

He interrupted. "Get to the point!"

"Well — What if I suggest that all the girls —" she

149

corrected herself — "women, I mean, Jessica and the others, wear mauve and white checked *doeks* in the synagogue and then — I'll put it into Sal's head so she'll think it another of those different ideas for that novel scheme of hers — have all the Indian waiters wear the identical sashes?"

"You've got it!" he said, grasping her hand and congratulating it. "Oh, Ceza, I think we've got it — !"

He left her abruptly and lay back, worn out but spirited.

Which was so like him, she thought: angrily helpless and therefore masterful.

Presently he said authoritatively, "Yes. Yes yes Ceza. It's perfect. Perfect. The perfect feminine touch." Overexcited, he paced the room.

"It's beginnings that concern me. Note plural — beginnings. You understand, I know!" He struck his chest furiously. "Ceza — it has got to be begun —"

These days they often talked about this. She said soothingly, "I know."

But an irritated movement of hands compelled even more than her usual enthralled attention. "My passion is with beginnings, not destruction." He spoke more slowly.

Slowly, as if it were a litany, he said again and again, "My passion is with beginnings, not with destruction."

She moved towards him and settled his head on her breast. Her fingers trickled through his shiny dark hair. All Indians have greasy hair except Indra, she thought triumphantly and for the thousandth time, knowing that it was one of those important things that ought not to matter.

"Ah," he said, almost regretfully, she thought, "You are so good for me, Ceza."

She merely dribbled the edge of her nails along his scalp.

"And why are beginnings my passion?" he asked rhetorically. "Because there is not one political party here, or for that matter, anywhere, that deserves any respect. In any case, all opposition here is in the form of polite, pretentious and therefore ineffectual debating societies. Or, better still, declaiming societies expounding on the brotherhood of mankind, as if illusions like brotherhood and justice and humanity are all that is needed to mean concrete evidence of change. As if no one knows that people are more important than theories! Spare me," he said fiercely. "Save me from that! Listen," he tugged her hair, "Listen to me, Ceza. If I can't have the ballot box, then I'll have the match box... Believe me, I am no fanatic. But if fanaticism means the detestation of theory and analysis, and a belief in results instead of explanations, then I am a fanatic. I refuse to listen to all the excuses about why the Defiance Campaign — prayer-days nothwithstanding — failed, the way I would refuse to drink the tea made by the Liberal Party ladies at the Treason Trial." He stopped and said half-teasingly, "You're no liberal lady, are you?"

"Not if you say I'm not," said Ceza. She knew she must encourage him to speak, to let some of his bitterness free.

He continued. The mordant edge to his voice sharpened, but did not quite cut off that lilting lullabyish accent of his. "What have all our Congresses and even the Congress of the People, those disorganized, indolent but articulate debating societies ever done that could possibly disrupt the aristocracy? The aristocracy, or as they would say in one of those clever slogans of theirs — white man's overlordship — what d'you suppose was the effect of the bus strike on them? A few were moved to profound sympathy and allowed their cars to be used as chariots in which to carry those weary black walkers, those misguided dreamers who thought that the voluntary proximity of the nobility meant some kind of breakthrough. Ah, but you will tell me my conscience is the conscience of the rich, because my mother is a silk-pilgrim, because my silk-lined pockets are full to bursting, like my heart. I therefore have access to a conscience — that dangerous weapon that is denied the downtrodden, the poor, the over-exploited. Conscience is antithetical to helplessness. I am shamed and they are shamed — but our shame is not the same — they are shamed because they obey. And if obedience is not complicity, then what is it? Oh, I know they suffer from malnutrition and that that deprives them of energy. I know they have a gigantic inferiority complex — tell a man every day that he is inferior and he will believe it — tell the same thing to an entire people and they will embrace it. Lace it all with tribal divisions, brilliant informers, theoreticians and an efficient military regime, and what do you have? Millions of obedient victims whose only honest denominator is a failure in courage. Heresy, you'll say? Certainly this is how those debating societies will see it — and the liberals would rather see pity than truth . . . But the masses and, it sometimes seems to me, their so-called jargon-using leaders fail to see that the strength of power is equalled only by the strength of their cause . . ."

He flung himself away from her. "But you understand,

152

don't you, Ceza?" He laughed bitterly. "You agree, I'm sure." He went on, "At bottom, you could blame all this on Hitler—or on the Jews. Take your pick—it all depends on which side of the fence you find yourself. Why? you say. Why? Because together they made racism unfashionable. No one seriously believes that India would have won independence in the way it did if there had not been the Second World War. The same is true of the free countries of this continent. This is something, without doubt, that must not be said to the bourgeois liberals in our midst; it is not something they care to understand, though our enemies know perfectly and understand perfectly. They know there have been more oppressive regimes than this one, and that these have been overthrown. Can the liberals, for that matter, can anyone say that this is the most oppressive regime there has ever been? The Hungarians would disagree, I'm sure . . .

"We have policy-makers instead of leaders. It's the passive policy of evasion that I resent most of all. Where are the disorganized expressions of anger that should have come about if only because hopelessness nullifies danger? Why has there been so little violence against the overlords?"

He interrupted himself, "Someone has to ask these questions!" He continued relentlessly, "It is not a case of these over-obedient victims being deprived of rage as well—they've more than enough of that! My real quarrel with them is that they allow their hard-earned rage full license among themselves: ask Neville—he'll tell you that the kind of injuries seen in black hospitals, multiple lacerations, for example, are not seen anywhere else! Injury is too mild a term—battle-wounds would be more appropriate. They do battle with one another instead of with their overlords . . ."

He stopped suddenly and tugged Ceza's hair again. "But I am of them, and it is we who do battle with one another, we who indulge in internecine strife because we do no more than direct our bravery against one another."

"Oh, Ceza," he said violently, "Ceza, don't you see?" Now he struck his fist against his chest. He said, "I can no longer endure my humiliation!"

His voice caught, and he collapsed in sounds that were a collision between a sob and a shout. She'd known him to abandon himself in sound before, when they'd made love and were at that end of his that so often and so deliriously coincided with her own. She contained her ends internally from the beginnings; not even a sigh escaped, for in her clasping concentration she over-rode everything, and even sound. And now it was as if he had taken her inside his very innermost noises, as if he had trusted her with all the breath he had . . . For a moment or two she lapsed into them, into those noises that had lost touch with control, and understood that nothing is more intimate or more consolidating than involuntary sound. She looked at him then and it was as if she had happened on the scene of some awful accident — her mind travelled back to the night she had rescued Jacob from the police, back to the sour smell of his terror, and back to his shame. Because her shame had been blindingly new. She said, "You must let me help."

"*Yes?*" he said, regaining himself. "*You?*"

He began to speak as if he were giving voice to entirely new ideas. "Perhaps you could help after all," he said thoughtfully. "The Lieb-Gordon wedding would be our target."

As he began outlining his plan his voice gathered a speed that went with his thoughts. Weddings are venues for so much beside marriages, he told her somewhat ponderously. He assumed that the guests of honour would be the two cabinet ministers whom she'd told him had been invited. They were, if his memory served him well, the Minister of Bantu Affairs and the Minister of Economic Affairs, and, if he wasn't wrong, both of them had important business connections with the Liebs and Gordons respectively. These two dignitaries were, he believed, natural targets, easy too; as long as there were no organized cadres to torpedo things . . . Clearly a team of three, he predicated, a *team* mark you, and not a group, but a team of three such as himself, Ceza and Neville were in a position to eliminate all risk. Indeed, guaranteed secrecy. He was certain of the infallibility of the formula he had devised and to which he now addressed her; prohibit any and all form of membership, and outlaw any and all form of calligraphy. He would put it more simply for her — no writing and no gossiping and therefore no informing. He explained that Neville's engineering device meant that he was able to manufacture a miniature micro-wave device — he had access to the necessary equipment . . . It would be very small, the size of a packet of cigarettes, but large enough to detonate a parcel. He would present a parcel to the ministers, he would lay it in front of them and Neville would set it off. There must be a moment when all her family would be away and safe — he was sure they would have their photographs taken. She told him he was right. She went further and told him that there was, in the City Hall, a room that was set aside for precisely this purpose — the photographer, Bealsley, had undertaken to arrange the

155

flowers in there for himself. He was pleased about that, he said gravely, because he knew how she felt about her family, it was one of the reasons that had made him have so much respect for her. And of course, if he wore a mauve and white checked turban — her most inspiring idea! he would, by virtue of his anonymity, be unidentifiable. And averred, in that endearingly impish way he had, that she knew it was popularly said of an Indian that when he wears his fez he's Daddaby, and when he takes it off he's Patel. He thought it seemed a foolproof idea. Even so, Neville and he would engage in a full-scale enquiry. In the meanwhile, she was to think carefully . . .

It was not long before she heard those other sounds of his that owed everything to achievement and nothing to despair. She could not do enough for him. Nor be enough.

He slept.

Her mind tossed and turned.

Abruptly, she woke him. She said, "Why don't we burn your blazer? I refused to own one — remember?"

And in his kitchen sink the small fire cast their naked shadows in shapes that reminded Ceza of music notes, she saw quavers and crotchets and even the treble clef. The smell that rose and embraced them might have been incense. Indra, her idol, was now forged into a sacrament. Once more she longed — in the manner of an incantation — to say, "Indra, Indra — I'm going to call you 'I' — 'I' for Indra and 'I' for me."

She would help him: his cause was her cause and at the edge of her skull there beat Ruth's declaration — ". . . thy people shall be my people, and thy God my God." She felt as brave and Biblical as Ruth . . . For the attention she gave Indra's plan was more in the style of prayer than thought. But inside the third eye that sees beneath the skin she knew that intelligent level-headed thought was the one impediment she dared not permit — an impediment that had anyway been disposed of as if it had been a childhood disease. He trusted her at last and in his trust she found her validation.

7

These days the telephone at Villa Evermor rang persistently. As soon as the Liebs unpacked a gift or opened an envelope the result was immediately transmitted to the Steeles. Philip had developed a new joke: "Only tell me about the cheques — the rest is women's nonsense!" he'd said. Later, when Philip had said "Cash is king on Broadway," the nature of the gift was abbreviated to: "A king or not a king?"

Irene and Ceza were in Philip's study when the phone rang.

"Ceza —" Philip said. "Put your mother on."

"Are you all right?"

"No. Let me speak to your mother."

"It's Dad," Ceza said.

"What's the matter?" Irene said almost automatically, for his tone rather than his words had come through to where she'd been standing.

"Listen. I'm going to speak very softly. I don't want Ceza to hear me. Got that?"

"Mmmm —"

"Now don't ask any questions. Except this one. Ask me whether I've seen the doctor yet —"

"But —"

159

"Ask me whether I've seen the doctor and then listen like you've never listened before. We're in terrible trouble. I'm on my way home — Ceza must not move anywhere. Don't tell her. Ask about the doctor, —"

"Has Dr. Solomn seen you —"

"I'm on my way home — One of my men's driving me. I couldn't drive if my life depended on it."

"Just get home quickly."

Irene jabbed the bell. "Your father's ill," she said. "They never answer bells around here —" She jabbed the bell again. "What's happened to everyone?"

"I'll fetch someone," Ceza said.

"No. Stay where you are." She added brokenly, "I don't want to be on my own —"

"Madam called?" Jessica said.

"The master's not well. Get his bed ready. He's coming home. We'd better get some lemon tea ready —"

"Will you tell me what's happened?" Ceza said.

"Dr. Solomn's sending him home. He sounded terrible. It's not like him — it must be a real emergency — he's not even driving the car himself, and you know how he hates to be driven."

"I'll go and call Jacob."

"No. Don't move. I'll ring the bell. Jessica or Jacob'll come."

Jacob appeared with his usual silver tray, iced water and headache powders. "Ow, Madam," he said. "Jessica, she tell me the master's sick —"

"I'm very worried, Jacob."

Ceza said, "Let's wait at the gate."

"He'll waste time letting us into the car," Irene said. "The front door is so far from the gates!"

"Outside the front door then," said Ceza.

"Come along Ceza—"

"I was just going to phone—"

"How can you even *think* of phoning anyone—"

"I was just going to phone Dr. Solomn—"

"He's on his way, too. My head feels as if it's going to burst."

They were appalled when they saw Philip—pale, sweating, shirt unbuttoned, his gallbladder scar seeming to jet out from his skin. He wiped his face with a crumpled letter. "I must get to our room," he said.

Irene tried to take the letter from him. "You need a hankie," she said.

"Don't touch that. Give it to me at once—" Philip held fiercely to the letter. The phone rang. "Don't answer that phone. Irene, tell everyone to say I'm ill—Then come back at once." He began to run up the stairs.

"You mustn't run, Daddy," Ceza said.

"Don't you worry about me—"

Up in the bedroom he began to arrange his bundles of keys as methodically as always. "We'll have a little calm around here," he said. "Where's the tea?"

At that, Jessica walked in. "I knew you'd do this for me," he said gratefully. "I could do with it."

"Shouldn't you get into bed?" Irene began tentatively.

"Bed?" he said incredulously. "Bed. No time for bed. I'm not sick. *Not yet!*" He sat on the bed. "Bring that chair up, Ceza. Irene, you bring the other one. Take the phone plug out, Ceza. I want no interruptions whatever. That's right." He added coldly, "You look pale, Ceza—"

"Philip, what *is* this?" Irene asked impatiently. "You're driving me mad—"

"In my own time, Irene. I'll handle this my way—"

161

"Well, you needn't be so terrifying —"

"Irene, you'd better listen. And listen good. I'll tell you what I'm going to do now. I'm going to read you this letter from Sarah Goodman. It was delivered by hand."

"For God's sake, get on with it —"

"Now, Irene, don't raise your voice. That's not going to help anyone, is it? In my own good time, I said." He spread his glasses. "You're very quiet, Ceza —"

"Yes."

"I'll read it. But first let me tell you — categorically — that I'll tolerate no interruptions —"

"Philip," Irene said. "We're not a board-meeting."

"Did you hear what I said? I don't think so. I'll repeat myself. No interruptions."

"We agree," Irene said nervously. "We agree. The way you put things, we'd agree to anything —"

"Well then, I'll begin.

My dear Philip,

I've already put a letter in the mail to Ceza, but I don't suppose she'll receive hers before you receive yours. Actually, I hadn't meant to write to you at all, but remorse is a relentless progenitor. I hardly know where to begin.

I'd better tell you what I've done.

I've become an informer.

{Here Philip looked up at Ceza, briefly. The rest of the letter was read without a glance at anyone.}

I've sent a letter to the immorality squad. I should tell you that by the time you receive this I shall be no more. I am to be thoroughly cremated, without, mark you, the benefit of any religious rite.

162

I informed the police that your daughter, Ceza Mavis Steele, is carrying on an illicit affair wth an Asiatic student (Hindu), one Indra Patel of 55 Cross Street, Fordsburg, Johannesburg.

I don't know why I did this. A pinch of madness, some malice, a handful of stupidity — a dollop of concern for your daughter — the recipe eludes me —

However . . .

I don't really know why I'm letting you know. But I have the feeling, a certain *frisson* you might say, that there is more to this than I know. You'd better interrogate your own daughter before the police get round to it; you may even have to leave the country. One never knows.

I wouldn't dare ask your forgiveness. You may yet thank me, though this is the last thing I intended.

Yours in sorrow, Sarah Goodman.

"She's a vicious evil liar!" Irene said at once. "My God — we'll have to sue —" Then her nails held her thin hair from her head; hillocks showed on her scalp. She was rushing on, "I don't give a damn about the publicity."

"Irene . . . Just a minute — Ceza?"

Ceza felt a disturbance about her loins. Otherwise inanimate. But for the pulse which beat with uncontrollable speed against her temples, her face was motionless.

He said again, "Ceza — ?"

"She's shocked! Can't you see she's shocked?"

Philip covered his face. Then he reached over and touched her temple. He said once more, "Ceza —"

Her silence was absolute.

He shook her shoulders — perhaps for help?

Irene called out, then moved to stop him. She said

angrily, "You'll hurt the child. Stop it — For God's sake, stop it —" She looked at Ceza then; a look that was so blinding that Ceza was forced to open her eyes. Irene said gently, "Ceza, you must tell us the truth —"

Philip took the cue as she had expected. "Your mother's right, Ceza. We want to help you. This is no time for recrimination. Listen to Daddy —" He hesitated. "Are you listening?" he said.

Ceza whose eyes had once again snapped shut, nodded.

A look, quick as a reflex, passed between the parents. Now Philip was authorized to take over.

"Ceza. This is no time for shame. We'll stand behind you, whatever you've done. You've got to speak to me."

"D'you think she's killed herself?" Ceza said. They looked at her — even her voice sounded disembodied, as if it had been sent across undersea cables.

"What are you talking about?"

"She killed Whyte. Sarah killed Whyte."

"Whyte?"

"Her servant. Twenty-two years of his life —"

Philip interrupted. "Ceza, we must keep to the point, Ceza —" His body sagged. "Don't push me too far. I'm doing my level best for control." A wince tightened his entire face. He'd seen too much. But he said firmly: "Irene, fetch the Bible you carried when we got married."

The Bible was where it always was — a mother-of-pearl ornament on her bedside table. She handed it to him.

"Now, Ceza, you'll have to swear on the Bible that you are telling the truth — on your mother's life, on yours and on mine. With what seems to be left of mine you'd better not take any chances —" He put the Bible inside her hands, then folded them, as if they were asleep. "You must answer my questions. Think very carefully. Take your time. All I can tell you is that we are your parents and we'll stand by you whatever you have done. D'you hear me?"

She nodded again.

"Good." In one of his rare moments of affection he covered her hands with one of his. "We love you," he said. His grip tightened painfully. She cried out. "I want to pour my strength into you . . . I'm going to ask you some questions. You've sworn on our lives — remember? Do you know this Indian?"

"Yes."

"D'you know him well?"

"Yes."

"How long have you known him?"

"Forever—"

His negotiating capacity, that inexpressible power of the double-bluff, in which his mastery had been proved again and again, flew faultlessly to his lips, "I'd better warn you, Ceza, that I know more than you think—"

Irene's weeping sounded so much like that unseen woman in Cross Street, Ceza thought. Mindlessly, she said, "What did I ever do to Sarah Goodman?"

"We'll think about that some other time," Philip said efficiently. More conversationally, he asked, "Have you given much thought to what it would be like — for you — in gaol?"

A loud oriental wail escaped from Irene.

"Save that for later," Philip said coldly. "Later, for visiting days—" He went on imperturbably. "He lives in Cross Street, doesn't he?"

"The library," Irene muttered. "All those trips to the library."

"I'm not angry," said Philip incredulously. "I'm too horrified for that. We're in too much trouble. I'll have to think very very quickly." Again he fastened his hand too stringently on both of hers. She winced. "Light me a cigarette, Irene, will you? And Ceza, if you think a firm handgrip hurts, the wardens will teach you to think nothing of ten times more pain! Either I'll tell you, or you'll tell me . . . You'd better talk quick."

Irene's weeping continued. "Stop that!" Philip said nastily. "There's still time for us to plan. Later, Irene, we'll cry together." He added urgently, "The passports?"

"Up to date," Irene said gratefully.

"Thank God."

"Passports?" Ceza repeated. "Passports?"

"Of course. We may have to leave at once. Tonight if there's a flight . . . It will depend on what Ceza chooses to tell me . . ." The art of his experience gleamed in his eye. "Ceza, the police have already been to see me. You remember Huys? The one that used to be in charge of store security? He's a big shot with the Special Branch. He owed me a favour, he said." A glance, hasty, but obviously authentic, was flung at his watch. "We've got exactly forty minutes left. After that, it's over to him. You can put yourself in his hands or in mine. I don't need to tell you that I'll be behind you whatever you choose." He stood up. "My considered opinion is that a father can do more than a stranger for his own child. What d'you think, Irene?"

"Ceza," Irene said slowly, "Ceza, darling, you'd better tell us everything — You'll always be our daughter. No matter what. Have we ever let you down? We've always been so *proud* of you — you know that . . . Don't put us in the position where we have to let you down. We're all in this together." She turned to Philip. "The child looks ill. Fetch her some water—" The bathroom was adjacent. When he'd left, Irene knelt beside Ceza. "Trust us, trust us," she said soothingly while, with the crook of her index finger, she caressed Ceza's temple. "Trust us. Go on, trust us."

That her parents now, for the very first time, asked *her* to trust *them,* shocked... But for her fluttering temple she was still. She had a sensation of great distance between eye and socket. Then, ineradicable swallowing. So far as she thought of anything, she thought of swallowing.

"Ceza," her mother said emptily. "Ceza— You love this — this Indian, don't you?"

Philip made an attacking sound. He said, "Shit — Shit — Shit —" He bit his knuckle. "You'll always be our daughter, Ceza." Not in vain had Philip relied on those sudden flashes of inspiration that were at the root of every brilliant lie. He said, "Did you know that — that... I don't know what to call him bad enough... swine... has given a detailed affidavit to the police?"

"He never loved me," she said. "You can't ask a man for his love, he said —"

"The child's having a break-down," Irene cut in. "Philip, for God's sake, can't you see she doesn't know what she's saying?"

"She knows all right. That's what he said in the affidavit." Irene made a sound like a mashing bell. "*Irene!*" Philip said desperately. "Can't you use your brains? *You* can go mad later." He turned to Ceza. "Listen, my girl, and listen good. You'd better tell me everything. If you like, your mother'll leave the room—" Ceza's head shook very fast. "No, you don't want that, I see..."

"Oh, no—" Ceza said. "*No no no no —*"

167

Philip went on thoughtfully, "Most of the people I know will think *I* ought to be shot — never mind you. I know human beings. D'you think I could have got to the top if I didn't know how to predict human beings?"

Ceza began.

Words, her words, were spilling in, she knew, these pale disfigured sounds that seemed to talk about things that were not so much disconnected as unremembered — so utterly unremembered, indeed, as never to have been . . . She was more aware, as if under cellophane, of her father's bowed head, of her mother's scalp, of the interior decorator's familiar dove-greys. Once or twice she stopped, and Philip, without raising his head, told her to go on, to get it over with: there was so little time. Beyond fear and outside terror, but very conscious of those flawless lawyers of her familied trust, which even now floated about her in their same immemorial presence, she knew that whatever else she had been with Indra, she had never been safe. Her father, she realized, could not focus his eyes on hers, while her mother stared at her in a stage-struck trance. A mess of her own dismay, the kind that numbs one into action, propelled her to speak as slowly and clearly as if she were trying to recollect filaments of a dream.

"You're leaving the most important thing out," Philip said. *"What about the politics?* That — that swine must have been using you for something other than the usual?" He smiled dreadfully. "You've done enough! Don't lie. Don't lie —"

And so their details of the Lieb wedding came out.

When Ceza had done, Philip asked quietly, "Is that all? Now are you sure you've told us everything?" But his tone emphasized and affirmed that he was satisfied that he knew all he needed to know. He said, "Start packing, Irene! Stop crying and start packing." He began to pace the room; his gallbladder scar had turned a deeper purple. "Get me the phonebook," he said efficiently.

"Philip," Irene said firmly. "You're thinking too quickly for me—"

He whipped a brief impatient stare. "You must be mad," he said. "Already mad. We're leaving the country — first flight out. To London — to the place my mother always called home. How's that for a joke — hey?" He laughed as if the sound were not meant to betray his disgust. He said, "We're in terrible trouble — the whole family." He stopped still, folded lips and arms tightly, and said, "Ceza's been good enough to tell me *her* plans. Now I'll tell her mine—" He marched purposefully to the door and locked it. "Now, Ceza, *you* had better listen to *me,* and listen good."

He'd decide later what would be done with the business — it might have to go public, after all. Still, there were worse things; they wouldn't starve, he could still provide a living for his family. They'd have to invent a convincing story — illness? Ceza was not to be allowed from Irene's sight, not for one second . . .

Ceza did not even try to comprehend anything about Philip's planning, or the speed of it all. She could not erase her parents' expressions from her mind: it was as if she had taken that one final last look and she felt she was chief mourner at a distant but frightfully important funeral. But it was as if her parents were finally wounded — so deeply did she mourn the light she had put out . . .

She felt grief; she felt naughty because she'd been found out: she felt so much that, for the moment, she felt nothing at all.

If time lost all relevance for Ceza, she knew that it was four o'clock if only because Jessica served tea. She sat in her parents' bedroom and watched Jacob bring the suitcases in, she heard her father arrange their bookings (they were to leave on the first plane, shortly before midnight), the bank manager was to step out of line (the traveller's cheques were to be signed at home, and not at the bank; the bank manager would deliver them himself). The doctor was expected (he'd be dealt with, as easily as the rest, he was Cosmos Stores' medical consultant, after all). He'd have no trouble talking, suitably gravely, of Philip's sudden rare and severe illness — Philip could count on him to supply him with the name of the most eminent consultant in the realm of the more mysterious diseases. The lawyer and the accountant were expected, too (it wouldn't have done to have left them out: they needed to believe they were in Philip's confidence and so he'd inform them, personally, and in the strictest confidence, of his illness). At any rate, none of them was to know the truth: the doctor would require some sort of explanation — Philip would hint something about a threat to Ceza. The god of superstition had decreed to Philip that if anyone's health was to be taken in vain, it was to be his. In the circumstances his health hardly mattered any more; the risk therefore was not too great . . . These professionals whom Philip had always regarded as irritating details, rather than people, had to be dealt with very quickly, though not obviously, of course; their sense of importance had to remain intact. Philip was good at this.

Neither Irene nor Ceza was allowed to leave that dove-grey room that had once been so peaceful. The clothes that were to be packed had to be brought there — Jessica and Jacob knew exactly what was to be done. They'd been told that it was winter in England.

Philip locked Ceza's bedroom door.

In a short time he'd found and removed what he was looking for. *How does one get rid of explosives?*

Well, he had no choice. Another phone call. The telling call that he'd been weighing and dangling since he found out... Huys... He'd phone Huys, the chief of the Special Branch. He'd tell him to come and see him. At least he knew he was not required to *ask*... All his life he'd distrusted revenge — it clouded and complicated thinking, so it was well that his action would now be based on nothing but necessity. Hadn't his mother told him that revenge was "forty-nine per cent present consolation and fifty-one per cent future punishment"? There was no time — perhaps he should not phone? Future punishment, he realized, was a euphemism for bad luck. He'd framed those words in his mind — now there was no possible alternative — he had to phone Brigadier Huys. He remembered Sarah. Brigadier Huys would know all about it tomorrow, in any case. Philip would use his material powers of persuasion and Huys would have to use his influence — what was all this nonsense about revenge? Huys would expect him to expect vengeance. But Philip knew that no fate that could ever befall that swine could even get close to vengeance.

The timing of the visitors was perfect as had been necessary. All had been as understanding and as concerned as they needed to be. "Tell your daughter," Brigadier Huys had said, sympathetically and disgustedly, "tell her we've got our — expert ways — to fix that black bastard." And Philip could not blame him when he added, "Ugh, Phil, I never thought I'd live to see the day that I'd pity you. Ugh! Tell her that she's lucky she's your daughter. Too damn lucky to deserve it! Man, if you weren't my friend this would be still worse for you!" Huys put his arm on Philip's shoulder, "I always said this is the sort of thing that happens when you let these buggers get too rich. Man, Philip, that coolie's father could buy and sell *you* and forget he'd even done it! Put that in your pipe and smoke it, man! University is not for girls, man!"

But Philip could only act — thinking would come later. Activity, mercifully, absorbs the brain just enough to prevent thought.

Then Jacob told him that Jessica had handed Ceza a special delivery letter.

Philip rushed into the grey room. "Who's that from?" he demanded.

"Sarah Goodman."

"Give it to *me* at once."

It didn't as much as occur to Ceza even to try to resist; in any case she felt attached to her father's pupils.

Philip read:

My dear Ceza,

There is no really good reason for me to write to you (and to struggle at the typewriter at that!) and yet in mitigation — as Louis would say — I could plead that

172

since I am now only your former mother-in-law to be, I have, at least, the licence to be honest and open with you. Yet I daresay that when you have read this your *real* and lifelong entanglement with me will have only just begun, though of course I will not be around to witness it. Dying of a chronic incurable disease so skilfully self-inflicted! I find — and not without at least some surprise — that the only person to whom I have anything real to say is you.

I know you, you see.

Yes, you too have been inflicted with a mind, no matter how much of a surprise *that* has been. *N'est-ce pas?* So, before I tell you how I know you, I'd better tell you that I like you, that if you had not been *not* in love with my son, we would probably have become real and gifted friends.

But Indra, you will think, she can't know *all* about him, about my carmenned forehead, about that transporting bed. But yes, I do know, Ceza — I do know about this thing that devours you.

Let me tell you immediately how I knew, or rather what induced me to find out. And at the risk of sounding sentimental, it was simply that you began to glow only after your engagement had been cancelled. You will be pleased to know that I have left very clear instructions that the ring is to be sold and you will be even more pleased when you know who will be the beneficiaries to the tune of several thousand — Whyte's children! — I do digress — forgive me. Anyway, you glowed. More than that you were edgy with your luminosity — and too erect. You had been pretty — you became beautiful; when I last saw you — you didn't see me, of course — you were even more beautiful because you had been chased with the tool of insecurity, because you had begun to realize that being white and Jewish and rich did not mitigate against your being no more than biologic, that not even youth or beauty or brilliance could defend you. And your breasts were no longer tagged on like postscript apologies, but became fuller. And I knew, could not help knowing that someone else had restructured you into being. And in that, you have felt yourself blessed. Even I might have blessed you, even though you'd rejected my son. But you chose the Indian and that was too much. Much too much.

Which you know. And if intelligence proscribes tears, it does not do the same for anger. You blush. Yet your blush ought also to be for me — the injustice was first perpetrated by me . . .

Evidence. Lawyers always require evidence, as their wives inevitably cannot know. And I think now, that all the petty injustices that made up my way of thinking were all committed in the name of being a good wife. How so? I was chosen, I knew, for that potential and only for that — it is this, you know, that informs most marriages, that exceeds all other nebulous qualities like love, looks and natural fit. And in my world (not too different, I suspect, from all those other worlds) a good wife was a simple equation — viz: Husbands first. But what is a husband? There are many breeds of course, but in my case a husband was defined in a career. He looked to his career for solace, excitement, for sensuality and validity and was not disappointed. I was the conveyor belt to facilitate all this and more — the belt on which could be laid those

174

other accoutrements for career: wife, child. One child, like one wife, was enough to vindicate his debt to society. There is nothing quite like the price-tags of responsibility to demonstrate that it exists. So the career was first, and Paul and I, so to speak, provided its tooled and leather spine. And therefore I became — though only with Whyte's help — an excellent as well as an economical cook. Whyte was with us on the very day that we returned from the standard honeymoon.

But I must get to Paul — I shall in more ways than one — return to Whyte.

So I had the husband and found I didn't much care for the career, either. Still, putting the husband first meant that one had to present all the outer evidences of being utterly fulfilled. One could not therefore pursue any of the odder interests of one's own — interests like studying something irrelevant to home-making — so one studied floral art, a little French, or bridge, one went to economical coutouriers, — innocuous things to show that one had no need for a mind, or a room, of one's own . . . This was the important thing. But, you see, Ceza, if one has a husband in one's life one needs a man as well. And husbands and men, I have found, are not necessarily linked. Accordingly, Paul became the man of my life. He would be the kind of husband I had not known I would have liked to have had. He would be interested in The Arts.

Sometimes, one lives by secret — and through secret. You, of course, know all about this, don't you? Secrets help if only because through them we give palpability to the great secret so improbably in store for all of us. Secrets are our private mysticism, and through them we conquer the damnation of boredom. And now that I am about to confront that improbable secret I wonder whether I shall continue to bore myself. When you're bored with yourself you become intolerably inquisitive about others. And who could be more interesting to me than my son's future wife? I've wondered about her since before Paul was born, and the strange thing is that you would have been right for him! A practised or self-spy such as I finds it astonishingly expedient to let free, to expose something of my arcane inner tumblings, to share by affliction whilst indisputably free of all consequence. It's not abatement I'm after. — If I *am* to die in peace, I'm to live a few last hours in peace, too. And I feel closer to peace than I've ever been.

What if I had been, say, an Indian wife?

And then, as remorseless as mortality, there is Whyte. Did you know that it was I who took the "I" out of White and changed it to "Y"? Not that I ever succeeded in taking the "I" out of "My." You see, I've digressed again; Louis's always hated that, it was hardly *comme il faut,* was it? But I feel so — so *conversational,* convivial, you might say. I have not been able to convince myself that I believed the chicken-mushroom pie was entirely safe when I gave it to Whyte. It's expiation I'm after, but only by all honourable means and so, Ceza, believe it or not, but honour dictated that I write your father, though I must admit that when I wrote that letter this morning, a century ago, I didn't quite know why. In all the world it was a servant, and only a servant who had never let me down. It seems I am, or have been (no matter) the kind of person who measures loyalty in terms of servitude. This was something Paul half knew, I think.

And so my confession is in your hands but my expiation is not yet complete.

Paul.

I'm still worried about Paul. So, a brief word. He's come a long way from being a son-man — my instinct tells me that. To do this he had to do three things. He had to leave me, and abandon gynaecology; above all he had to embrace his own heart — the heart he could not touch until it had been quite scattered. You did the third, almost willingly, I think. *I* did the first, unwillingly, and drove him away without knowing the wisdom of it. Perhaps, one day, you'll show this letter to him or at any rate see that he gets it. Were he to feel in any way responsible for my self-induced end, peace will be forever denied you. Not to mention me . . . You may yet become my posthumous daughter-in-law. What young bride ever knows such good fortune!

You've read this far. Some day some perspective will come to you — it will take some time. I leave to you the length of time that was meant to be mine, but which I choose to tamper with — As soon as I've been to my little post office to send this off by express mail to you, I'll return to my over-crowded empty bedroom where I'll avail myself of all the equipment I'll ever need. My gun has a silencer.

I'm only mildly curious about Louis' reaction. But curious.

Yours in womanhood, Sarah.

"Christ," Philip said, overpoweringly calm, "Christ. Have *you* read this, Irene?" He didn't wait, but rushed on. "Of course you have. You look as though you've — I can't tell what you look like! We'll all have to hurry up — it's almost time. You'd better get on the phone to say some goodbyes. It'll look bad if you don't."

"Yes."

Irene picked up the receiver, but instead of the expected dialling tone, she heard an agitated "Hello — Hell — o."

She said, "Mr. Goodman? I mean Louis —"

"Irene — I'd like to speak with Ceza —"

"I'm afraid she's out."

"Then I'll have to ask you to give her a message for me. I mean from Sarah."

There was a long silence. Irene was constrained to repeat, "A message from Sarah?"

Silence slowed everything in that grey room.

"You said you had a message from Sarah," she said.

"So I did. She left a message."

"Are you all right, Louis?"

"Hardly. Sarah's dead by her own hand. She died not five hours ago, I'm told. She left only one note. All it said was, 'Tell Ceza.'"

"Oh, my God! I'll tell Ceza as soon as she comes back. How terrible for you! We're about to leave for London. All of us. Philip is gravely ill. We're going to see Sir Emlyn Jones, a Harley Street man —" Irene spoke falteringly. Inventing illness had the finality of invoking one. And yet the words had come. "I'll tell Ceza as soon as she comes back. I'm so very very sorry. I wish you a long life."

"Thank you, Irene. They do wonders in London —"

When the receiver was safely replaced and Louis' words reported, Irene said, "I hope she only left one note. That's all I can say —"

"We're leaving in ten minutes," Philip said. "We must all change. Can't you see that the most important thing is to get out of here immediately?"

None of them knew how Irene had made her phone calls, still less how they'd arrived at the airport. Somehow Ceza had managed to say a very quick good-bye to Jessica. Ceza looked immaculate. Irene had made her comb her hair and put on make-up in the car. The Liebs arrived just as their flight was being called, foreshortening their tragic moments.

Once they were in the air, Ceza fought to draw her mind together. What had Philip said about Indra, about how Huys would deal with him, how easy that would be? *He won't trouble us again, Ceza* . . . What really engaged her mind was all that it had been able to grasp — Indra had sent in an affidavit that had incriminated her. Would she never see him again? "I" for Indra, and "I" for me . . . A streak of compassion for Neville passed through her. But why and how had Indra done this to her? To them? Only a few hours ago the answer had been unthinkable — now, it was all too clear: Indra had bought himself immunity at her family's expense. It did not occur to her to doubt her father. Because she had not known Philip to lie to her — she did not think of applying the same test to Indra — in trusting him, there had been no need for her to trust herself.

She should have told Mrs. Visser whom she could have

trusted and who would have brought her to her senses in time.

Because nothing had prepared her for this, nothing.

Was he in prison, then? No, of course not, she was his indemnity.

Yes, a few hours ago all this had been unthinkable. But now it was like a long-harboured and long-hidden disease, revealed suddenly, but at nature's leisure.

Then she saw that Sarah had been right: she had never felt safe with Indra. Indra had wanted her to know insecurity and to suffer — that was how she'd become something other, whenever she was with him. Indra had turned sin into exaltation when he'd calculated, from the beginning, on desecrating her parents, on destroying her. Somehow, with the help of what she now saw as having been sworn anew to sanity, she'd invent the ways and means of making it up to them. She would never make it up to herself. Shame, like emergency, procures special skills. Skin and blood counted — how could the wrongness of Indra's blood have been precisely that which had made it right? She believed she had never been as rational as she was now. She saw further: Indra had used his perfect affinity with her body. And still further: Indra was incapable of an honest emotion, leave alone an honest thought.

Reality — the skin-tight and only sensible kind — was within her reach. She'd leave the world of the mind to its rightful inheritors.

The merest suggestion that she needed a psychiatrist would do more than lessen her shame and her parents' disgrace — it would save them all.

Indra and Neville waited for Ceza. Once Indra had said that he could set his clock by the punctuality of her visits.

Neville's gratitude to Indra, though endless, was not burdensome. Still, giving it tangible expression was gratifying, and now listening to Indra praise him for having attended to his side of things so speedily, he perceived a slit in the thick shroud of self-doubt that he had clung to for so long.

"Ceza said you would produce the thing with maximum efficiency and in minimum time," Indra said.

"And you, of course, needed convincing?"

"I did you an injustice. I'm sorry."

"That's OK."

It was then they heard those unmistakable thumps, those unspeakable voices. Brigadier Huys did not wait for the door to be opened.

"Your warrant," Indra said.

"Save your legal talk for the courts. *If* you get there . . . I think," Huys said, "I think I'd prefer to have you seated. A rich coolie like you."

Huys waited.

"It's bloody hot in here. It stinks. Open a window." He said again, "It stinks in here."

"So it does," said Indra. "Now."

"Rudeness won't help." Huys flourished some papers. "Now, Ceza Mavis—" he paused as if to read—"Steele —Now she was not rude. No. She was charming when I saw her off at the airport. Pretty girl." He looked at his watch. "She must have landed at Heathrow."

Indra looked at Neville then, a look of dazzling humiliation. More than disbelief, his look foretold the kind of

181

pain that nothing can silence. He said, "That white liberal. That passionate Jewish liberal."

"He could be lying," Neville said.

"Grow up—"

"You're all the same, you people," Huys said. "All the same. Always. Savage to begin with; extra savage when betrayed."

PR 6055 .S4 B56

Eskapa, Shirley.

Blood fugue